RIDE A BRIGHT AND SHINING PONY

Editor: Clarinda Harriss
Graphic design: Ace Kieffer
Cover and interior art: Elisabeth Stevens
Author photo: Patricia Arvin

BrickHouse Books, Inc.
306 Suffolk Road
Baltimore, MD 21218

January 1, 2013

Distributor: Itasca Books, Inc.

ISBN: 978-1-938144-10-3

Printed in the United States of America

RIDE A BRIGHT AND SHINING PONY

Elisabeth Stevens

"We are a flash of fire--a brain, a heart, a spirit."
Thomas Wolfe, *Look Homeward, Angel*

"Man is not merely a possibility of recapture or of negation. If it is true that consciousness is a process of transcendence, we have to see too that this transcendence is haunted by the problem of love and understanding."
Frantz Fanon, *Black Skin, White Masks*

The Day Before

The Trailways bus comes into Washington, D.C. through streets lined with decaying red brick houses. Arriving from the North in August, our silver coach slid past grassless front yards where blacks rested beside ancient, wrought iron fences. Torn green shades swayed at curtainless windows, and in narrow alleys, beer cans rusted in stagnant puddles of left-over rain.

One of a handful of whites in a bus crowded with blacks arriving for the March, I welcomed the familiar streets. My name is Cynthia, and it was 1963 – the summer I was thirty years old.

I'd begun to anticipate seeing Lester as we passed the city's first outpost – a motel. Ten miles from Lester. Then, through the bleak stretch of pines that looked black against the six o'clock sky, I'd pictured him reading in his battered armchair by the window.

By the time the bus had reached the second landmark – the crossroads with the Hot Shoppe's Restaurant – I'd been sure he was thinking of me too. The communication was real—not fantasy. Sometimes in his apartment I'd called him with a thought instead of a word.

The bus turned the next-to-last corner. I welcomed the soot-stained Central Public Library and the down-at-the-heel park that surrounded it like old friends. It was an area of seedy bars, "$2-A-NITE" hotels and derelicts who gathered outside the sleazy sex movie across the street. It was also Lester's territory: he knew it as only a newspaper reporter could. A month earlier he'd investigated the murder of a wino in the parking lot behind the movie.

That area was my back door to Lester's world—the place I left New York behind. I was a researcher for a Manhattan history book publisher, but I had dreams of doing something active—even courageous.

The bus ran the last light, swerved into the terminal, lurched to a stop at a concrete restraining block. I helped the black woman beside me take a roll of posters from the overhead rack. One slipped out and we had to roll it up again. I caught the bus driver, a squatty little white man, eyeing me as we did it. "For Freedom We Have DIED," the poster said, "For Freedom We Must LIVE!"

By the time I'd gotten my bags together, the bus was almost empty. I always took too much to Washington because I wanted to stay forever. My biggest suitcase was crammed with paperbacks; novels squashed freshly pressed clothes and weighed me down like a mule.

"Marching tomorrow, Honey?" The driver demanded, making no move to help me as I dragged the bags down the bus steps.

I didn't like his insinuating drawl. "I'm visiting my fiancé," I told him primly. That was an example of my worst self right there— lying about being engaged but at the same time sounding self-righteous as a school teacher. I thought I'd eliminated that self after the divorce from Frank, but sometimes it came back like a rash or an allergy.

"A pretty little gal like you," the driver said, leaning so close that I felt the heat of his Sen-Sen breath, "could get herself killed," he paused, "accidental like." He drew a breath that was almost a sigh, "—running around with all them niggers."

He came a little nearer. His eyes slid down from my face to my body – exploring the folds of my skirt like a sticky finger. It was the same stare that had infuriated me in Italy on the unhappy honeymoon journey with Frank. Equal parts hostility and lust, the look erased all but flesh—imprisoning you in a suddenly-humiliating female stereotype that was just as impossible to contend against as "nigger."

"Honey—"the driver began wheedlingly. The word came at me like a curse. I pulled the last suitcase down to the sidewalk, scraping the bottom on the metal treads. "I'm *not* marching!" I told him with clenched teeth. Then, moving fast in spite of the bags, I walked off without looking back.

Safe beyond the wall that separated the busses from the front of the terminal, I wondered whether that last about marching had been a lie. I wasn't sure. I was sympathetic, but the thing didn't mean much to me. I'd seen headlines about an historic March on Washington for Jobs and Freedom, but what mattered was seeing Lester—not just for the usual weekend but for nearly two weeks, my vacation. Besides, history was something you verified and organized in an air conditioned office—not anything that could happen to me.

In front of the terminal, there were taxis waiting. Washington wasn't like New York. Taxis were plentiful, and drivers even carried your luggage. I gave the man Lester's address and settled back—relieved to be riding because each block was bringing me nearer to Lester.

When we stopped for a light on Fourteenth Street, the driver turned around and stared. He was white, wizened and sixtyish with skin the color of tobacco juice and hair that was dull reddish brown and looked dyed. "Sure you want up here?' he demanded. "Bad part of town—Park Road. You got the right address?"

I told him "Yes," but I knew what he meant. Lester lived in the center of the black section—if it had a center, spreading almost all over town as it did. The summer before, Lester had taken the apartment simply because it was cheap and he owed his father, a farmer, for the year of journalism school behind him. Now that the debt was paid, to stay in the apartment had become a question of honor. Sometimes Lester did talk of moving, but most of the time he was on the other end of the argument—worried because he, a liberal Southerner, was living in the only white house on the block. Just a few weeks before, he'd been downstairs when prospective tenants came and been embarrassed to have to say the landlord would only rent to whites.

It was a good two miles from the bus terminal to Lester's block, and he was even farther away from places like the Washington Monument and the Lincoln Memorial. We went straight up Fourteenth Street past white pillared funeral parlors, nightclubs outlined in blue neon, all-night laundromats and "Karry-Home" food stores. At the corner where a big

People's Drug Store squatted like a slab monument to shininess, we turned right, passing the old Tivoli, a Moorish style movie house that was decorated with blue tiles and still played double—sometimes triple--features. The Tivoli's side doors faced a Safeway that was bigger than the People's—a shopping mecca for the six or seven blocks around.

Like others in the area, Lester's block was shabby-decent. No broken windows or garbage-strewn front yards—just three and four storey row houses set above small, tiered lawns. Most of the fronts were stuccoed or shingled and trimmed with down-at-the heel colors such as grey, ochre or dusty orange.

I singled out Lester's house as soon as we passed the Safeway. Some houses had small, cone-roofed turrets covered with flaking paint; others had sagging second storey porches supported by squatty Doric columns. Lester's though, was the only one with a Tuscan dormer window. The window, sheltered by the overhang of the red tile roof, was only a few feet from the bed.

It was a little before seven. As we slowed down, the breeze brought me soft, late summer, twilight smells. Warm tar in the street and meaty suggestions of what people had been having for dinner.

"—the middle of the block—"I told the driver, but it was too late. The alarm was ringing in the two storey stucco firehouse that stood half way between Lester's and the Safeway. The jangling continued; the street's somnolence was transposed into specious calm. Blue-green fire house doors cranked up; red warning lights flashed. We were forced to wait while two engines swung into the street and careened—only half a block to a house just a few doors beyond Lester's.

I could see the light in Lester's window. I expected at any moment to see him look out. "I'll get out here," I told the driver, not wanting to wait.

I opened the door, paid the driver, dragged the bags out before he could help me. The cab slid away, and I was left on the curb with my things. The fire house lights stopped flashing; I saw the sun setting in a brownish pink sky behind the Safeway. Down the street where the engines were, there wasn't any smoke. Half-expecting to see flames spurt from a window, I was at the same time certain it was a false alarm.

I gathered my bags and made a bee line for Lester's door. I wouldn't have to use the key he'd given me, I fantasized. Parting like the unlocked gates of dreams, the brown-rimmed, glass paneled, white curtained double doors would open. Lester would be standing between them, his arms outstretched.

I got as far as the three concrete steps that led to the scraggly front yard, then one of my bags opened up. About ten books dumped out on top of my best underwear. I had to squat down on the sidewalk and stuff everything back, so it wasn't until I was struggling with the last, weak clasp that I saw Lester.

He had closed the double doors behind him and was standing on the stoop facing where the fire was supposed to be. He frowned—I got the feeling he couldn't make up his mind about something. Then he tightened the belt of the old tan raincoat he was wearing and set out across the yards like a streak.

I called, but of course he didn't hear me over the sirens, and he was half way to the magenta-colored house where the engines were before I could struggle to my feet.

For just that instant—kneeling in a pool of shadows under two trees, I got the quick, funny feeling that I was a spectator crouched in a pit below a broad stage of surprises. An enlarged and somehow unfamiliar Lester was crossing the stage with the wide-footed Texas stride I knew so well. It was as if I had come unexpectedly on a hidden part of his life.

I stood up; the pink beam of a revolving fire engine light struck me. I shielded my eyes and saw Lester disappear into the house three doors down. There wasn't a wisp of smoke, and two people Lester knew—a red-haired fireman and a thin, dapper black man—were standing on the front walk chatting. Still, I didn't like it. Lester had told me how he'd once been nominated for the Carnegie Medal for Bravery after saving someone during a Texas tornado. However unlikely, the idea that he might try to save someone from a fire scared me.

I was almost sure Lester wouldn't like it, but I made up my mind to follow. Just then, though, Edmund Williams, a black man who was the most successful person on the block, came by on the way home to his house up by the Safeway parking lot. Edmund Williams insisted on helping me get my things to the stoop. Then, almost before I could thank him, he nodded gravely, picked up his expensive-looking attaché case and was gone.

At that moment—I was standing on the first step – I saw Lester coming out of the magenta house with the black asphalt roof. If someone hadn't called him, he would have seen me immediately, but he turned back to answer a voice that sounded as if it were coming from the bottom of a chimney. I couldn't make out the words or what he answered, but when he came down the walk, his face was white and set.

I saw him say a few words to the dapper black man named Walter and wave at the red haired fireman named Jim who was rolling up one of the hoses. Then a window banged up and a dark form leaned from a second story window. I couldn't see anything but a lot of hair, a barrel-like arm and the curve of an enormous breast. "—and you just watch *yourself*—" the same roaring voice I had heard before shouted. A hand gleaming with rings waved a rude dismissal, the sash slammed shut. All three men had turned to look—was she talking to Lester or one of the others? I never did find out, for just then, Lester saw me.

The first fire engine was turning around, its red warning light revolving. One shaft highlighted Lester's resentment—even hatred— at being caught unawares. Then, in the instant of dimness before the next beam, that expression was masked, and on the next revolution, softened into something else. He became roseate, and with each flash, increasingly joyful.

Escaping the small crowd that had gathered on the sidewalk, he broke into a boyish, ingratiating smile. But even then, that first, half-frame flash still lingered. Like a negative after-image, I still saw his first instinctive start—the Southerner surprised by the momentarily superfluous and unwanted woman. Even as he waved, ran towards me, called my name, I was stabbed by the certainty that our love was doomed. He was on his front walk when the fire truck slid past us, clanging like over-loud background music, but it seemed that we were balanced and opposing warriors facing each other over a long, sand-colored distance.

There was no transition. Our time apart telescoped; I was crushed against him. He blew in my ear, chucked me under the chin and wooed me with words all at once. "—and my poor baby was just standing here like a little old lost lamb—my *goodness*—"

He led me up the stoop. He swept the double doors wide before us. He drew me though the vestibule and into the hall. He was carrying all my things but still had a free hand to hold me.

"A false alarm?" I asked—almost the first words I said to him.

"Of course, baby, of course."

He set down the bags and kissed me. Aware of the pleasantly familiar odor of his raincoat, I repeated the comforting words. "False alarm."

The hall had a battered table where they left the mail. In the spotted, gilt-edged mirror that hung above it, I saw his winsome, slightly irregular face. His nose had been broken in a fight over a girl when he was fifteen, but he had clear blue, appraising eyes and a wide, inviting smile. He was 27, but his leanness and the lock of dark, wavy hair that hung down over his forehead made him look younger—almost a boy.

He kissed me until I was out of breath. There was a dusty,

one bulb chandelier in the shape of a star above his head. I felt him expanding. His energy made the light brighter, the yellow flowered wallpaper less faded. A last fire siren wailed and then subsided; we started up the uncarpeted stairs together.

"—that's the second false alarm she's turned in this week," Lester was saying.

"Who?"

"Esther, hon, I've told you about her before."

I was sure he hadn't, but we were at the first landing, and it was beginning the way it always began. I was not the same person who had watched him from the walk; I was being drawn out of myself and into him. It was like being sucked out to sea on a warm, slow current.

"Old Es," he went on without leaving time for a question, "I guess when she gets drunk she thinks everything's burning—or else she just figures it's time to get the boys at the fire house up to her place." He laughed.

"I was afraid you might get hurt," I told him. "What was she saying to you?"

Lester smiled. It was hard not to believe him when he smiled. "Nothing much, hon. Just some drunken thing. I went in to tell her that if she was fool enough to turn in another alarm, the police'd pick her up for sure. She wouldn't listen though—locked her door and wouldn't even let me come in."

Lester did small favors for people on the block sometimes, and they came to him with requests about matters where the influence of the paper might help. I wondered why Lester had gone to seek Esther out—was he beholden to her in some way? I wanted to ask him, but we were already on the second flight—leaving the closed doors of other people's lives for the third floor that was ours alone.

"I was beginning to worry your bus might have been late," Lester was saying. He unlocked the door, dropped the bags inside and looked around. "I must have dropped your coat somewhere—no—don't go—I'll get it."

He went down and I walked in. Home. *Home.* Even the smell was familiar—a warm mixture of empty beer cans, books—Lester's enjoyable personal aura. Ever since the summer before when I'd separated from Frank and met Lester, my real place had been in that apartment.

I stood in the kitchen facing a sink full of dishes. The window was open onto the flat back roof where we sometimes sat facing alleys and the downhill expanse of neglected back yards that were yellow-green in summer, brown in winter. The sink faucet still leaked. The two blue plates and the three green ones were waiting for me to wash them. Half a dozen of the glasses I had brought from New York were there too. The dishes suggested love—not work—the small, sensuous enjoyments of taking good care of Lester.

During the two years I'd been married to Frank, I'd hated housework. "Woman's work," Frank jibed when I occasionally begged him to help me. He was busy—he had male, important things to do. But with Lester I enjoyed scrubbing the patched and pieced linoleum with a mop I had bought and sweeping (there was no vacuum) the brownish-pink rugs that never quite looked clean.

He came back with my coat and kissed me. We shut the door and went through the small middle room that contained the eating table, a battered bureau and an ageing sideboard. In front was the bed sitting room where the dormer window faced the street. Lester put my bags in the corner by the closet. Then he took off his raincoat, and we sank into the big, raunchy, red sofa that stood where the ceiling slanted in under the roof.

The rest of the room contained Lester's large, dilapidated armchair with its badly fitting green and white slipcover; a baronial, black, carved table that he used as a desk, the dark, mirrored bureau marred by the bottle rings of previous tenants, and a high-backed, over-decorated walnut armchair suitable for a deposed king.

Facing us, projecting into the center of the room from a wall uncertainly covered with spotted pink paper, was the soft, loose-springed double bed. The first time I'd come to the apartment, I had thrown the sleazy, pink-tufted spread into the corner of the closet because it suggested other lovers. A year later, it was impossible to imagine anyone else sleeping in our bed.

"Oh, honey—I've missed you—" Lester let his neck go limp; his head rested on my shoulder. Then he sat up again and faced me. "If I hadn't known you were coming tonight, I could've bottomed out with a real case of the miseries." His eyes searched my face. "You didn't write last week—"

"You didn't either—" I countered.

"With the March coming I had to work seven days straight at the paper. I didn't get a day off till Sunday, and then it was too late. Most likely a letter wouldn't have reached you."

The March—I wanted to forget it, the bus driver and everything but the comfortable evening that lay ahead. "I didn't write because the Korean War book went to press yesterday," I said quickly, conscious that our conversation was stiff, a little strained. It was as though we first had to set aside the days we spent apart so we could savor the meat of our lives—the days we spent together. "We were rushed all last week," I told him. "Now everybody says we've run out of wars."

"That won't last—" he stopped, shifted. "Some folks think we're going to have one right here." He paused again. "Cynthia," he said, slipping his arm along the back of the couch behind my head, "are you coming tomorrow?"

Right away I thought of the big yellow building down on Pennsylvania Avenue where you went for a marriage license. In odd moments in the previous week—standing on subway platforms and

18

waiting for elevators—I'd been nurturing the dream that Lester and I would go downtown and get married on the day of the March because he didn't have to work. We'd honeymoon until my vacation ended, I'd fantasized, then I'd go back to New York and give notice at work and move out of my apartment.

"I'm going to be covering the March for the paper," Lester told me, "so I thought we'd—"

I couldn't let him finish. "But when you called a week ago Sunday you said Melvin Anderson was doing it. You said they were giving you the day
off."

Lester's hand lingered on my head for a minute, stroking the hair he always said was the color of buckwheat honey.

"Melvin still is doing it, baby, but in the beginning they didn't think the thing would get so big. Yesterday they decided to assign somebody else besides. Five or six guys wanted it, but they gave it to me because Melvin said I could do it best. He's their top black reporter, so they usually go by what he says. They like what I've been doing lately—wait—you haven't seen these." Lester went over to the built-in shelves under the small skylight that lighted the middle room. He came back with a tan envelope full of clippings and emptied it onto my lap.

There wasn't even time to give my dying dream of a getting married a decent burial. Like a swimmer caught in a current, I struggled against him. Then a headline struck me like a searchlight. "POLICE CHIEF WARNS OF POSSIBLE VIOLENCE." I couldn't help reading that story, and then I started another: "Five thousand police and National Guardsmen will be on duty in Washington during Wednesday's March For Jobs and Freedom. A 222-man riot squad will be stationed in undisclosed areas of the city armed with clubs, tear gas and shot guns...."

Lester must have seen how I felt, because he took that story back before I could finish it, gathered the others up and put them on the little table in front of us. "Skeered?" he demanded, squatting down in front of me and patting my arm. "Lots of folks feel that way, but they're wrong. Melvin says tomorrow is going to be good, not bad. I think so too."

He stood up. He was dressed in white—just sneakers, a tattered pair of summer shorts and an old T-shirt—but the pale tones gleamed in the dying light; his tanned body glowed. I thought of the Mercury statue I had seen once in Florence and imagined small wings sprouting from his heels and shoulders.

"You don't have to stay to the side tomorrow;" Lester was telling me, "we'll march together."

Lester seldom let me come with him when he worked. To be asked was an honor, a gesture of love and confidence. Still, I hesitated. The anger had drained away, but I felt small, uncertain.

He came down towards me. "Don't you want to?" His eyes scanned my face. "It's just with you—" I felt his wings drooping.

It wasn't the time to say no. I let him carry me beyond myself. A ride on the wind. "I'll go," I told him.

He looked pleased and padded out to the refrigerator to get beers for both of us. Just as he got back, the phone rang. His face changed, he hurried to answer it, then stood with his back to me while he waited for what seemed to be a bad connection. Nothing happened. After a minute, he hung up.

"Who was it?" I demanded.

"Don't know," he said, not looking at me. "somebody—maybe an operator—said my name, and then nobody said anything." He turned, made a gesture as if to brush away shadows. Then, instead of coming back to his beer, he went to the small, overflowing bookcase beside the couch and stood facing the shelves.

I got the feeling something was bothering him. For some reason I thought of Esther, but before I could ask he was back beside me. "I got a new book, hon."

I felt restive—as if he were leading me into a blind alley, but I hated to interrupt. Books were meat and drink to Lester.

Lester's new book was the autobiography of Jawaharlal Nehru. "There's a fine line in the beginning," he told me. "'The journey is always worth the taking,'" he read slowly, "'even though the end is not in sight.' Good, isn't it?" He looked to me for confirmation.

"It could mean almost anything, couldn't it?"

"Maybe."

He caught my eye and something dissolved between us. I laughed at myself. "Always analyzing—ain't ya—" he said with a grin, dropping down beside me.

We were back to ourselves again. I kicked off my shoes and took the big pins out of my hair, letting it fall in the waist-length coil Lester had made me promise never to cut.

"Sometimes, Cynthia," he confided, leaning against me while I scratched his back, "it seems the farther I go the behinder I get."

"Why?" I demanded. "You put yourself through journalism school. You were the only person in your high school class to go to college."

"I know," he nodded, "I've come a long way—but nowhere near as far as I'd thought. In three years I'll be thirty, and then it won't be but a minute before my life is half over. Alexander the Great conquered the whole *world* before he was thirty."

Instead of laughing, I scratched harder and then hugged him. "But you'll win the Pulitzer Price," I told him, giving him back his favorite dreams. "You'll be an editor of the paper, and then maybe you'll go home and get yourself elected to Congress."

"I will—" he told me before he gave in and smiled "—if I get the chance—"

We drew closer; he relaxed against me. I began to feel better.

The March was only one day, I told myself, shutting out the fear of it. That left the rest of my vacation for leisurely evenings, quiet dinners....

"Two whole weeks, Cynthia," Lester said with a sigh, reading my thoughts.

"Twelve days," I said, dissatisfied again, knowing it would end.

"Long enough to make love a hundred times," he countered. "It's better than a weekend, isn't it?" He worked his arm behind my ribs, pulling me closer.

"Yes—" I thought of the year-long arrangement Lester sometimes called "a honeymoon every two weeks." Neither of us could afford the trip oftener, so what other way was there? One weekend a month I came to Washington; two weeks later, Lester came to New York. Saying good-bye Sunday nights was bad, but there was always another weekend twelve days away.

"What is it, baby?"

I hesitated. Part of me wanted to see Lester happy, untroubled by questions I was almost sure he didn't want to hear. Another part of me counseled that simply by asking, you could get what you wanted. Looking away, I saw my unopened suitcases sitting in the dark corner that had been light only a few minutes before. Then everything slipped out in a lump. "I'm tired of New York," I told him. "I'm tired of my job, and I—"

"Well, my goodness—" Lester began in the comforting Southern way I knew so well. He stroked my cheek, drew my head to rest on his shoulder.

I was close to crying—not just because of what I'd said, but because when we were apart my feelings coagulated. Glad to shut out what was left of the light, I buried my face in his neck, spoke to the warmth of his flesh. "Lester, I want to stay here with you."

Whiney as the words sounded, there was a certain relief in them. We had been talking—no, truthfully—arguing the subject all summer.

Even when I made resolutions, somehow it always came up. Like a blemish on an otherwise handsome face, it was the thing the eye of my mind returned to again and again.

"Well, maybe one of these days we'll just go ahead, honey," Lester said softly. He freed himself from me and stood up.

Watching my reactions like an actor, he went to the closet and took off his sneakers. Next, he stripped off his T-shirt and hung it neatly on a hook. Then, making his way easily through the half-darkness, he was back beside me. I forgot all about crying. His hands caressed, encompassed me.

The shabby room was part of the embrace—warm, familiar, comforting. As through a brown haze, I saw Lester's big bed. His eyes followed mine. "I put clean sheets on for us," he told me.

Our arms loosened, he rose before me. I knew he was about to carry me to the bed. I felt limp, emptied of volition. Like a sleepwalker groping for safety, I raised my arms so he could take me up.

Just then, the phone rang again. Lester frowned, turned, left me and went to the rickety little table beside the bed. Coolly, a little breeze came in the casement and took his place beside me.

"Billy? Is that *you*, old stud? What in tarnation are you doing in these parts?" Lester reached for the wall switch by the bureau and snapped on the light.

My heart sank. Lester had friends the way some dogs had fleas. They called in the middle of the night, arrived unannounced expecting to sleep on his couch, inevitably borrowed small sums which only occasionally came back—usually via money order. Women (from what Lester had told me) had frequently melted out of his life like raspberry ice—leaving nothing but sweet, pink stains, but the men stayed. I was afraid Billy would come between us.

"You *did?*" Lester was saying. "What kind of trouble?" In the ugly yellow light of the two bulb ceiling fixture, I watched him straighten, tense. He had switched to the hearty voice and down-to-earth language he habitually used with men. The gentleness he had with me was gone. "Well, *hell*," he went on, shifting from one foot to another, "why'd you have to go and do a thing like that?" There was a pause. "Well, I don't know—that's a pretty tall order—"

The conversation went on. It promised to be a long one. I was almost certain that the Billy who seemed to be asking for help was the college roommate Lester had told me about. Once Lester looked my way and smiled, so I waited, but after a while it was like air escaping from a balloon. When there wasn't any left, I put on my shoes and headed for the bathroom.

Lester saw me go, but he didn't try to stop me.

"Sure I'm still going with her," I heard him say before I shut the door, "I've got her staying here right now."

The words made the blood rush to my head. In spite of all the chivalry, Southern men were raised to consider women chattels—prize possessions like the sports car Lester dreamed of owning. Lester loved me and that made it different, but, knowing he would kiss away my anger later, I resolved that I wasn't going to have anything to do with Billy as long as he was in Washington—fix dinner for him or anything like that. If Lester wanted to see Billy, he could do it alone.

I went to the cabinet over the basin and took out the toothbrush that I kept there, brushed, spat green tooth paste into the running water. Happier, I turned to the open window and leaned on the sill which, like the rest of the bathroom, was covered with peeling light blue paint.

Beyond aging roofs and distant blocks, I could see the silhouette of the Washington Monument at the bottom of a long hill. For a while I just stood there, watching the lights flick on and smelling the coming night. The smell of darkness turned my thoughts to the summer before—the first night on the beach with Lester.

I'd only been separated from Frank two months then. Still

newly glad to be free of the destructive quarrels, I was empty perhaps, but peaceful. One Saturday, I was invited to a wedding. Aware of the irony—my cousin, who was ten years younger, was getting married while I was getting divorced—I accepted anyway and agreed to drive an unknown friend of the groom with me to the shore of Long Island. The friend was Lester.

At the reception, while I danced with the lawyer who was going to help me get the divorce, Lester watched, waited for me. Later, he told me he'd been jealous even then. When the cousin and her new husband pulled away in an old green convertible decorated with streamers, Lester and I were standing near a wooden fence in front of the house. We'd been drinking champagne, and without warning, he kissed me. I drew back—not from him but because people I knew were watching. People I'd never been able to live up to. People who'd never understood why I'd married Frank—a struggling photojournalist from a far-from-rich family. What will they think? I'd wondered, not even daring to look at Lester.

Later, when Lester and I left the wedding, I let him drive. I had a vague idea of finding a beach where we could swim, but soon we came to a place where the country road branched at a triangular knoll of grass.

"Which way?" he said.

"I don't know," I told him, "you decide."

And so he did decide, but before setting out he reached for my breast and kissed me again. It seemed natural that time. I didn't resist. And although I couldn't remember afterwards which road he had taken, I was certain we were going in the right direction….

Later, when it began to grow dark, we had never come to the beach someone at the wedding had suggested but were driving to the other side of the island. Then in a place that I would return to in dreams, we were crossing flat, grassy marshes on an empty road. It was there Lester began to tell me the story of the Alamo.

By then I'd gotten to like his accent and seen that he was handsome in spite of a faintly unkempt look—the ragged collar, the frayed tie, the little remnants of what looked like sleepy sand around his eyes. I listened to his story of the brave defense of the fort, caught up in it but at the same time aware of his exaggerations of the dramatic parts. There was something contradictory about him, I sensed, failing to put my finger on what it was.

Lester drove on and on through the warm summer night. It was late and dark and we hadn't eaten dinner. Where were we going?

With Frank, I would have been frantic to stop. He was rough and abrupt—rushing me in one direction or another without leaving time for rest or reflection. That night, though, I was like Frank—impulsive.

The wedding champagne elation was still with us when Lester finally found a beach. He kissed me again quickly in the car, then drew me out over the dunes. They sky was black. We clung together, stumbling through sand without being able to see our feet.

The beach was damp. A low, grey sea mist was drifting in like the paraphernalia of a dream. Our plan had been to go swimming, but Lester did not have a bathing suit. Mine was dutifully clutched in my hand. Were we still going?

After a few minutes of hiking across the deserted beach, we stopped. As though it were natural and fore-destined, we lay down. Soon he was helping me take off my clothes. My fancy dress for the wedding was wadded into a ball and tossed aside. My underpants were pushed down to my knees, and then I felt his big bare foot reach up and pull them off. The gesture seemed funny, and as he came into me, I was laughing—the sort of laughter that is involuntary—not planned.

The love making went on for a long time. It was like being carried on a wave. I had said only the day before that I did not want to even go out with anyone until I was divorced. I had been certain I wanted to be untouched, inviolate after the wild and destructive break-up of the marriage, yet I no longer cared. Thoughts and resolutions swept aside.

Afterwards, it seemed that we had come a great distance together—far further than from the wedding to the beach or from New York to the wedding. My resistance was nothing like that of Lester's Alamo. I had surrendered and was embarking unprepared on a long journey.

At last Lester drew me to my feet, pulled me toward the water. Naked, we met the waves, but as the sea touched my thighs I felt cold. While he bathed and splashed, I held back shivering, wanting to plunge in but afraid until he came to get me....

Lester was knocking on the bathroom door. "Honey? Are you sick or something?"

I opened the door immediately. "I was looking out the window. I thought you were still on the phone."

He led me into the kitchen and through the dining room that was lined with National Geographic maps of places like India and Australia—symbols of trips he (hopefully we) would someday take.

Lester brought me to the bed, but I was no longer ready. "Let's sit over there," I begged, so we returned to the red couch.

"Honey," Lester began, "that was Billy Mougin, my roommate from school, remember?"

I nodded.

"Well, you're going to get to meet him. He was up to New Jersey for business like last summer, and he'll be in town tonight. Seems he stopped for a hitch-hiker up the other side of Baltimore and got into a fight with him over some fool thing. Old Bill hit him one and then took off, but now he's worried he might have done the guy some damage.

Billy thought—since I work at the paper—that I could take care of it in case there was trouble."

"Could you?"

"He had no business skedaddling, but I s'pose I could so long as he didn't hurt anybody much. Most likely he didn't—Old Bill's a little out of shape. The only trouble is, there's more to it."

"What?"

"That's just it—he wouldn't tell me. Said he was calling from a Baltimore filling station where people could hear him and he'd have to give me the rest of it later. Most likely it's nothing much—all I hope is that the guy he hit wasn't anybody to do with the March."

"The March? But isn't Billy the one who never passed a beggar by—the one who used to share meals with you when you were both down to your last dollar? Why would *he*?"

"Did I tell you all that, hon?" Lester stopped, smiled. "Billy's spent most of his life in Texas," he explained. "He thinks like a lot of other folks at home. When I told him we couldn't see him tomorrow because of the March, he told me I oughtn't to be wasting my time at a Commie-nigger camp meeting."

"That's awful—what did you say?"

Said I thought he was short on facts and maybe I could give him some tonight. I told him we'd see him about midnight after I get out of work and—"

"Work? You have to work *tonight*? For the second time that evening, I felt betrayed. Yet I knew it was just like Lester not to tell me something unpleasant until he had to. Because I was a woman, he kept the sun in everything as long as he could—sometimes too long—until we were chilled by the shadow of the unspoken.

"It's only a couple of hours tonight, baby." Lester was eyeing me as if I were something that might explode. Later, I knew, he might make me laugh over it and remind me how I'd been "all puffed up."

"I'm not exactly the star reporter on that paper," he told me. "So when most everybody'd gone home, and they decided they needed a guy to do a man-in the-street, night-before-the-March piece for the late edition, I said I'd take it on."

"Where's Billy going to be?" I demanded.

"He's going to meet us at the Georgia Lounge. I said there because you like it. It's a celebration—Billy's wife had her fourth girl a little while back, and he's going to buy us champagne."

"Champagne?" I was moved by his enthusiasm. To Lester champagne was the ultimate. He'd given up hard liquor five years earlier after a New Year's Eve when he'd disgraced Audrey, his former fiancé, and been sick for hours.

"—and baby," Lester continued, "we've still got time together—it isn't even dark."

A half-truth. The sun had been gone at least half an hour, and the back rooms were crowded with white, summer night shadows. I hesitated. Should I resist, complain, tell him how what he'd said to Billy on the phone had made me feel? I noticed that the breeze had died with the light. The apartment was getting oppressively hot. I felt weak, as though embalmed in warm jello.

Sighing, I leaned against him, limply resting my head on his shoulder. "Oh Lester—I wish you'd tell me the *truth*—"

"I do, baby."

Our eyes met. I saw that one part of him was masked, calculating to counter questions, but another part of him was glass—I could see he loved me. "I didn't want you to cry, Cynthia," he told me softly. "I didn't think you'd mind so much about tonight afterwards—" His eyes lingered on the bed.

"Oh—" His kindness washed over me like warm water. I no longer wanted to take him to task or talk. I sighed again and fell silent, wishing we could go and lie together.

But instead he straightened and drew back. "Come to think of it, Cynthia, there _is_ something I reckon I ought to have told you—"

He paused, and for an instant, in spite of the heat, I felt cold.

"—I'd even thought about _lying_," he went on, "—making up some story or other and telling you not to answer the phone—but it wouldn't have been right."

"What are you talking about?"

"Honey," he moved to the edge of the couch, then stood up, "some tom fool in town thinks he wants to kill me."

I felt as if a huge mouth were sucking my blood. I stared at him. "_Why?_"

He shrugged. "Darned if I know." He half turned away and stared at the floor.

"Who is it?"

"Don't know that either." He grinned, shifted, trying to shake off the heaviness that weighed on him. "Whoever it was phoned the paper twice last week—only spoke to the operator, but next time they might call here."

"What did he say?"

"He—she—the person wouldn't talk in anything but a hoarse whisper—just said they were going to 'get' me and hung up."

"It's a racist who doesn't like your stories," I told him, remembering that one of the paper's best reporters had died several years earlier just as he was about to publish investigations of voting irregularities in certain Southern states. The reporter's skull had been crushed by a hit and run driver only half a block from the office. No one had ever proved that it was anything but an accident, but the coincidence was discomfiting.

"Maybe. It could just as well be a black who doesn't think the paper goes far enough. They get mad sometimes too—even though they know we're on their side." He sighed. "Maybe it's just some old crank talking to hear his head rattle." He drew a deep breath and faced me, squaring his shoulders like a boxer. "If anybody's going to try and get *me*, then he's the one who'd better look out."

A frail boast, but somehow I half believed it and smiled.

Just then, directly beneath our window, a bottle shattered. I stood up, but Lester got to the window first. He leaned out, scanning the street. "Walter?" he called to the thin, dapper black man who had been at the false alarm.

"—Lo there, Les." Walter raised a languid hand and smiled. He was lounging on one of the little steps that led from our yard to the sidewalk.

"You all right?" Lester demanded.

Walter flicked something from the padded shoulder of his jacket, then toyed with a fragment of glass with the tip of a polished, pointed-toed shoe. "Esther's still at it," he said laconically, barely raising his voice. "She won't let me home. Tried to nick me with a bottle from that window," he nodded at the house three doors down where the false alarm had been, "but she's too pianoed to hit the broad side of a fence." He turned and spat elegantly into a small evergreen.

"O.K. Take care." Lester left the window.

"What happened?" I went back to the couch.

"Nothing serious, just a little love spat. When Esther gets drunk, she won't let Walter near her. She's getting worse too—why last Saturday night—" He broke off. "Don't worry hon, the street's quiet otherwise. I thought tonight might be like a weekend—people out celebrating—but most of them are home. It's a good sign."

I nodded, thinking of the anonymous caller.

Lester looked at me. "Now nobody's going to hurt me," he said as if in answer. "I'm going to live to be eighty." He paused, grinned "—even though the best way to go is to get shot at seventy-six by an irate twenty-five year old husband. 'Why'd you-all make my little gal pregnant?'" Lester mimicked in broad dialect.

It wasn't one of his best jokes, but we both laughed.

There was shouting in the street. Lester went to the window again and stood there for a moment. "Esther's out there making as if Walter'd done every sin in the book. She's a hell kitty—told Walter if he didn't watch out she'd—oh well—" Lester smiled, shrugged. "Honey," he mused, standing before me, "why do you think she always says 'you *black* bastard'?"

"Maybe it's because, deep down, she feels the same way about blackness that some Southerners do," I volunteered, analyzing as always.

He game me a quick look. "Maybe—or else they're just reminding each other." As he spoke, he took the thin white cotton blanket from the bottom of the bed and draped it over the casement. The action was a symbol: he always put the blanket up before we made love—shutting out the street, the eyes of neighbors.

Instinctively, I got up. He did not have to call me. Like a trusting animal, I came.

"I've wondered lots of times," he said as we stood together, "— why *do* people hate black?"

"I think it's the *idea*—not the skin of a person," I essayed. "It's the color loss," I mused. "It's the color of defeat, darkness–death." Chilled by my own words, I paused.

"You're an idiot intellectual," he told me tenderly, taking me by the back of my neck and drawing me to the bed. "You think people can do things just by thinking." He pinched my rump. "You're wrong, old hoss."

I laughed. We sat down on the edge of the bed, and I took off my shoes. A part of me could have argued with him, but it had gone to sleep. The process that had begun on the stairs was complete. It was the reverse of the physical act of making love. Instead of his entering me, I was gradually, inevitably absorbed into him—thinking as he did, feeling as he felt. It wasn't the temporary confusion of two bodies making love—the uncertainty as to which was my hand and which was his. Instead, it made me think of the legend from Plato about lovers being reunited parts of the same person.

"Cynthia—" he burst out suddenly, "it's been so long—"

We kissed. He snapped off the light. I took my side of the bed without question—instinctively returning to the known, the home, the familiar place.

"I love you—" I answered, promising myself that I would die for him if necessary.

We lay naked together—open to each other—all barriers gone. Slowly, the passive enjoyment passed. I became an animal, devouring his body and encouraging him to devour mine. Had it been possible, we would have consumed each other.

I was carried far from myself. Blackness…. The word caught in my mind in the midst of pleasure. For a moment I thought I understood everything, then the intuition died in sensation.

Finally, when our long journey was over, he fell asleep without withdrawing from my body. Sometimes I liked to watch him that way, but that night I closed my eyes and followed him into darkness....

When I woke up. Lester was sitting on the side of the bed putting on his socks.

"Are you leaving?" I was afraid immediately—thinking of the threatening phone calls.

"I've got ten minutes, but I've got to get ready." He patted my shoulder, stood up to tuck in his shirt.

"What about dinner?" I said, knowing he would not eat but asking anyway.

"I'll get something later—don't you bother with me. Take

whatever you like from the icebox."

I smiled, certain I would find little beside bread, cheese, milk and maybe an apple. Lester hated to eat because he was afraid of getting fat. When someone served him a big dinner, he ate, but he was sorry afterwards.

Once he had been fat. I had seen a snapshot and knew how he hated that time. Like a calf to the slaughter, he had first been stripped of Audrey, his fiancé, then forty pounds, then his job. He had gone to Mexico to write and stayed a year in which he was unsuccessful, almost penniless. It was a time he was not going to repeat.

From the street, there were explosive shouts, then hoarse screams. "They're at it again—" Lester tied his shoes and stood up.

"*Black bitch*!" Walter's contemptuous tones cut the air like a raw tin edge.

I sighed, stretched, shut my eyes and listened to the comforting sound of Lester's footsteps moving from bureau to closet. The street fight seemed far away. For the moment I shared Lester's confidence. The voices outside grew softer, died.

Blackness. I thought about it again. It was the sort of thing people analyzed in school. Hours of reading and collating and note cards. Effort in some airless library. The black in American literature. Certainly Ph.D. candidates had devoured that. In black binders, their dissertations stood in neat rows somewhere. But what did such works have to do with the real story—or even stories Lester wrote every day?

"You asleep, honey?"

I opened my eyes. "No—just thinking."

"You think too much," he told me kindly. His hand lingered on my forehead, then moved down, stroking my eyes shut.

Frank had said the same thing, but the telling had been violent—never tender. He would shout, drink, pound the table.

Lester's hand left my head. "I'm going," he told me. "It's late."

My stomach contracted. Lester was standing above me fully dressed. He was wearing his one good suit and the blue striped tie I'd given him. He was his working self—dedicated, determined, busy.

I sat up naked and couldn't find my underwear.

"It won't be for long," he comforted, reading my face.

"You come down and get me at eleven-thirty, and we'll go have ourselves a good time."

Clutching one of the pillows to my body, I stood up. I was miserable—furious at my own weakness.

Gently pushing the pillow aside, he cradled me in his arms. "I love you," he told me in the softest voice imaginable. "Just a little girl—just a little girl—my *good*ness—" he told me in baby talk, kissing my face, wiping away imaginary tears, softly pinching my cheeks.

The completely familiar phrases made me strong again. "You'll be late," I said quickly, giving him a last kiss. "You'd better go."

"If I don't you'll get me started again." He grinned, straightened, scooped change and keys from the three-legged Mexican dish on his bureau. "Bye hon."

He went. The kitchen door slammed. I heard him run downstairs. I went to the window, took down the blanket, watched him go down the walk. Walter was still there, leaning against a hydrant and lighting a cigarette, but there was no sign of Esther.

Lester headed to where he'd parked his ten-year-old Ford sedan. Blacks greeted him as he strode down the block. As he unlocked the car, someone waved at him from a second storey window.

Wherever he went, it was like that. Lester drew people like moths. Gentle, unimportant people hovered in his aura. At work, for instance, there were copy boys and secretaries who idolized him. Certainly someday he would return to Texas and run for office the way he'd always said. But when that day came—where would I be?

I folded the blanket Lester had used for the window, dressed and went to the ice box. Contenting myself with a dry wedge of cheese and some milk, I went back to the front room and settled in Lester's big chair. Beside me, Lester's Nehru book was open on top of Conrad's *Nigger of the Narcissus.* Closing the Nehru, I picked up the Conrad, opened it in the middle and read: "The sea and the earth are unfaithful to their children: a truth, a faith, a generation of men goes—and is forgotten, and it does not matter!"

Chilled, I went out to the kitchen for an apple. When I got back, I wasn't in the mood for reading. Instead I just stared at the room as I ate—getting used to the place all over again.

Have you ever noticed how a person's place changes once they've gone out? You become an observer—almost a spy. The background comes forward—it's like being on stage between the acts. The set is there, but the play is interrupted, and—like oversized shadows of moths before the footlights—things that have happened haunt you.

Before I'd even gotten down to the core of my apple for instance, I was thinking about the time when Lester'd first told me why he'd broken his engagement.

"—and one night when I decided to go up the block and surprise her—" (I remembered the way Lester had paused, risen from the big chair to pace back and forth before the bed.) "I got as far as the gravel drive beside her house, and—"

He'd turned, come back to face me. "Audrey had a glassed-in front porch. I went up a little flight of wooden steps and then, right through the front window like a picture in a book—I saw them. The guy with her was somebody that lived around the corner—" Lester'd stopped, drawn a deep breath, turned away. "You know," he'd told me, coming back to sink into the big chair and shielding his eyes, "—to this day I can see just how they had their hands…."

A door slammed somewhere outside. There was running in the street. High heels clicked on concrete, but by the time I got up and looked out, whoever it was had gone.

I went back to the kitchen and made coffee. Then—I suppose because I was there all by myself—I got thinking of what I'd told Lester right after he'd confessed about Audrey.

One humiliation to wash away another—was that it? Anyway, it was then I'd told Lester about the evening—right after I'd separated from Frank—when I'd gone along to a New York party. In the middle of it—as though dragged by a magnet—I left. Alone and without telling anyone, I went straight to Frank's studio on the lower East Side.

His motor scooter wasn't at the curb, but I went up anyway, climbing stone flights that smelled of urine. At the sixth floor landing where there was a slit window opening on an airless well, I turned left. Passing the two hall toilets that served the floor's four apartments, I came to the cul-de-sac outside Frank's door. It was too dark to see my knees. I listened, knocked lightly, knocked again. There was no answer.

Without meeting anyone, I returned to the garbage-strewn street. There was no place I could wait, and I was increasingly sure Frank would not return but was spending the night elsewhere with a woman.

I had to see him, or, failing that, get as close to him as I could. Was that why, maybe two minutes later, I was standing on the roof panting because I had come back up all six stone flight—plus a seventh wooden staircase to the hatch?

The roof was flat. I went first to the far corner that covered Frank's apartment, my heels sinking into tar still soft from the day's heat. Then I stretched out on the cinders and cried. Then—I didn't do it without starting twice and shrinking back—I went in my black, high heeled dancing shoes down the twenty-five-foot long, steel fire ladder attached to the side of the old brick building. Jiggling from rusty bolts, it hung over a sheer drop to an empty lot containing crushed cans and cannibalized sofa carcasses. I went down to the level of Frank's sash tops, took to space like a poet to an empty page, swung across and over to his fire escape.

There was nothing to it. I smashed a window pane with the heel of my shoe, flipped the lock and was crying myself to sleep in his unwashed sheets in a moment. Of course he didn't come home. My companions were the indestructible roaches. I woke in the morning, found photographs of his new girl strewn on his desk amidst unpaid bills, wrote him a long, accusing and apologetic letter in pencil on the expensive paper he used for printing his photographs.

When I tiptoed out to the hall toilet wearing his raincoat no one saw me, but later, when I got dressed and left after eating his last egg, I passed the superintendent in the vestibule down by the mail boxes, and he laughed at me. Was it because he had seen Frank with the girl friend and knew I was nothing but the unwanted wife? A laugh like that is like getting cut on a paper edge. It's surprising that anything so innocuous can sting so much.

Of course the trouble with personal stories comes in explaining them. The difference between me and historians I knew at work was that they were able to reduce events to "Causes" or "Effects." With me, there was always the question mark—the sense that seen from another viewpoint what had happened could mean something different. It was like one of those faded family daguerreotypes you come across in an attic sometimes. From one angle you see the stiff, half-familiar ancestral face—but from another there isn't anything but your own shadow on aging glass.

I finished my coffee. Then, just as I'd resolved to unpack and begin one of my books, the phone rang. First I was afraid, then angry. If it was the person who had telephoned the paper, I'd threaten *him*. I stalked across the room, snatched the receiver, said "Hello," as loud as I could.

"Les Sullivan there?" an equally loud male voice boomed.

"No," I shouted, not to be outdone.

"Well this is his editor," the caller said in a slightly quieter tone, "where in hell is he? We need him down here."

I relaxed. "He left fifteen minutes ago, he ought to be there any time," I said in my normal voice.

The editor snorted. "I guess he'll be along then." He paused. "This his girl?"

"*Yes*." I was almost as strident as before.

He snorted again, seemingly expressing his opinion of late reporters and girl friends in general, then hung up without saying good-bye. Like Lester when I talked to him at the paper, he was too busy for amenities.

As I sank down on the bed to laugh, the screaming in the street began. I ran to look out and saw that a crowd had gathered, blocking traffic. The crowd bulged, parted; an enormous black woman broke from the circle. Broad-shouldered and straight-backed, she was ringed with layers of flesh. Graying hair hung to her shoulders in a thick, twisted mass. She screamed, she spat, she spewed back imprecations I couldn't understand at the crowd. Mounting the little steps leading to the front yard of the house three doors down, she raised a huge fist as if in warning. Then she ascended the walk and disappeared as if sucked by a whirlwind. It was the house where the false alarm had been, and without being told, I knew she was Esther.

No one followed, but the crowd grew more diffuse—spreading out from the spot where they had gathered. Then, at the empty space in the center, I saw the body of a man. It was Walter.

My heart pounding, I slammed the window shut and dashed downstairs.

I flung open the glass door to the vestibule—only to be stopped by Maria, the young Puerto Rican mother who lived in the first floor apartment with a handsome husband. They had only been married a year, but already they had a tiny baby. Sometimes I envied them. Their apartment was smaller than Lester's—one room with a closet kitchen—yet they seemed so happy. The Puerto Ricans believed Lester and I were married. I worked in New York, Lester had told them. Later, when my job was over, I would move to Washington.

"Don't go into the street," Maria begged, clutching my arm. The baby snuggled to her breast began to cry, his thin wails rising above the voices of the crowd.

I decided to be brave. It could be no more dangerous than the coming March, and if Lester could take chances, so could I. "I've got to," I said, freeing myself from her childishly small hand. "Lester isn't here—he'll want to put it in the paper." I opened the outer door.

"I too then—" Shielding the baby's eyes with gentle fingers, Maria followed like a soft shadow.

We went down the steps and into the milling crowd. In the midst of a loose, gesticulating group, Walter lay on his back on the pavement. He looked more emaciated than before. His light blue suit seemed too big, his yellow satin tie too loose. His mouth was open, his eyes had rolled back until only the whites showed. One arm was slung above his head, a brown finger pointing meaninglessly, the other clutched his chest.

It was a moment before I noticed the black knife handle protruding between his clenched fingers. He seemed to be bleeding from the back. As I watched, the pool of blood around him increased.

Was Walter really dead? The scene was overshaded, unreal. The street lights were blinding, the tar shadows were too black. Up the block, the little bulbs that formed the word "TIVOLI" flashed nervously against overshadowing night. Beside the parking lot, the red word "SAFEWAY" gleamed against blank concrete.

I hadn't seen a dead man since I was twelve. My eighty-year-old grandfather had lain among roses in a coffin lined with cream-colored satin. For three days, he had rested in his own front parlor—the expected termination of an ordered life.

Jostled forward by the crowd, I was standing at Walter's feet, facing the lightly scuffed soles of what were obviously new, rust-colored suede shoes. As I stared, a bubble formed at his lips. "Look—" I said to a boy beside me, pointing. "Is he breathing?"

"No ma'm—ain't nothing but left over air." He stared for an instant and then turned away as if he was going to be sick.

A siren sounded from Fourteenth Street, and the bubble broke. I went back to the curb where Maria was waiting with her baby. I no longer doubted that Walter was dead, but somehow, I couldn't take it in. All the wars I'd read about at work—even the photographs of corpse-strewn battle-fields—hadn't prepared me for a single passing.

In spite of the heat, I began to shiver and then, without expecting to, cry. Maria was crying too.

"Did you know him?" I asked Maria after a minute.

Between sobs, Maria nodded. "He no good," she said with a superior sniff that belied her tears, "half the nights he never come home—so Esther get mad, buy a knife."

I blew my nose. "Is she still in her house?" I demanded, trying to be as strong and logical as I knew Lester would have been at such a moment. "Why doesn't she run away?"

"I don't know," Maria shrugged. "A crazy one. Kill her husband, go home and cry. In Arecibo it happen many times like that. Woman sorry sometimes, but the man dead."

Sirens screaming, a police wagon pulled to the curb. Three policemen got out. Roughly, they nudged the crowd aside. A young black girl was knocked to her knees.

"You can't do that!" I began, springing angrily at one of the policemen. But before he even noticed me, Maria pulled me back, forcing me to sit on the curb.

"Don't say like that to the cops," she warned. "They get mad, you know. A friend of mine—that way she get killed—"

I felt weak. No longer capable of shouting, I was glad to sit hunched on the curb beside Maria and her baby, passively allowing my view to be partially obscured by the crowd.

Beyond the high-heeled patent leather shoes of black women and the gleaming brown and tan shoes of black men, I saw the black shoes of policemen surround the body. The dead hand—the only part of Walter I could see—disappeared. Only the blood remained. At first shoes skirted the mark, but then I saw dark red on a black rubber heel.

Covered with a grey blanket, the body was raised high on a canvas stretcher. The green doors of the Police truck slammed shut. The motor started, the siren resumed its wailing.

"Where will they take him?" I asked Maria.

"The morgue," Maria told me. "I went there once. We think my brother was killed, but he wasn't. People there in big ice box drawers. They pull them out by the handles."

Two policemen stayed behind. Swinging their clubs, they ordered the crowd to go home.

One cop caught sight of me and stopped. "What are you doing here?" he demanded roughly, ignoring Maria.

"I live here," I lied.

He gave me a hard stare and passed on.

"He thinks you live with a nigger," Maria whispered.

I knew that Maria considered herself white; still I was flooded with a sense of shame. Not at the suggestion that I might be married to a black, but at the unfairness of the policeman's prejudice. "I am black," I felt like shouting after him, but of course it would have been ridiculous.

Maria and I retreated up the three little steps that led to our front yard. "Look," Mariah said, pointing, "they go for Esther."

In step and swinging their sticks, the two policemen had arrived at the house three doors down. I saw that two police cars, appearing silently and without sirens, had cut off the block. Policemen were standing in the street, and the two original cops were mounting the small, stuccoed stoop of the shabby, three storey house. The cops rang the bell and waited, then rang again. When no one answered, they battered through the plate glass door with their clubs.

Then the screaming began. In the second floor of the building, moaning echoed as if from a cave. I thought of a huge creature—a bear, a buffalo, an elephant—imprisoned in an airless cell. The cry rose and fell. The sound was more disturbing than the sight of Walter's body. It was the voice of animal injustice, inevitable death. Like a sea rising over sand prints, it erased ideals, words, history.

A torn green shade snapped up. A second storey window banged open, raised by two heavy black arms. The arms reached out over the sill like a drowning swimmer's. The fingers spread, clenched on air. Then, as if snatched from behind, the arms disappeared.

A minute later, the two policemen came out. They were carrying the enormous woman between them.

"That's her," Maria whispered. "Esther. They take her," she added, "—but she be back."

Esther struggled, bit, nearly broke free. She was wearing an orange dress that scarcely covered her elephantine thighs. One foot was encased in a hoof-like, square-toed pump—the other was bare. Before they threw her on the grass to pinion her wrists and ankles, I saw her fingers dig deep into a policeman's neck, leaving a bright welt across the throat.

By the time they got her to the police car in front of our house, she was quieter, hanging like a barrel between them. Her head lolled back so that she glared at us upside down like an obscene Medusa; grey snakes of her hair scraped the payment.

For a moment, her eyes seemed to focus on me. "Tell your sweet man he'd better get my bail," she shouted in a hoarse, torrential voice.

"Tell him if he don't I'll—"

They swung her inside the car and shut the door. Her face pressed wildly against the window for an instant, but then someone inside pulled her back. The squad car swerved from the curb and we didn't see her again.

I turned to Maria. "What did she mean?" I demanded. "Was she talking to me?"

Turning so I couldn't see her eyes, Maria hesitated. "Maybe Lester—maybe he—" She glanced at me quickly and shifted the baby to the other shoulder. "I know nothing," she said softly.

"But Maria—"

The sirens began again. The rest of the prowl cars moved away. When I turned back to question Maria again, she disappeared through the doorway like a gentle shadow.

Traffic began to flow through the street, and slowly, the crowd dispersed. Someone turned on a radio loud in the window of a first floor living room, and the quick, happy, superficial dance music echoed through the heat and growing darkness as if death were nothing at all….

When I got back to the apartment, I sank down on the bed and picked up the phone. At first the newspaper's line was busy; then, when I rang back, there was no answer at Lester's extension. I left my name with the operator and—not wanting to sit and think—paced from front to back, went to the toilet, unpacked. Then, mechanically, I washed and dried the dishes, wiped the dining table and set out the plates for breakfast.

Finally I found myself examining the contents of the closet; a graying sneaker from Lester's college days in which a mouse had kept her family for a week before I'd discovered them; the reddish brown suede jacket Audrey had given Lester their one Christmas; the striped wool poncho he'd bought after that in Mexico when he was eking out a miserable living as a free lance writer. In Mexico (I remembered

Lester's unhappy confession) there had been a young girl who believed Lester would marry her, but when she begged him to come with her to a priest—

I shut the closet door. Then, back in the middle room (I was still waiting for the phone to ring) I started looking at the things Lester kept in the battered sideboard with the broken door. A half box of cards left over from Christmas. Check stubs, diplomas, his Air force wings. An unused photo album and envelopes of snapshots. There was even one of Audrey (she was a somewhat flashy brunette) that had escaped his destruction of everything to do with the engagement.

Then, in the center compartment where the door hung on one hinge, I saw unpublished stories Lester had written in Mexico stuffed in under an old, wadded up pair of dungarees, I took the dungarees out and folded them (their smell was male, familiar, reassuring) and tried to fit the perhaps twenty typewritten manuscripts back into the blue cardboard box where they belonged.

The box collapsed. Unused paper spilled out on top of the manuscripts. (Lester had given them to me to read, and most were about proud, sensitive men with names like Tex or Big Jim who fell in love with beautiful, unfaithful women and ended up wanderers in a sad and lonely world.) Then, in the bottom half of the box under a thin piece of cardboard, I found one story Lester had never shown me.

It was called "Speed," and I sat down at the table in the straight chair that was nearest the phone and read it. The story told of a man who, after a "mendacious respectable period as a salesman," became a Formula One racing car driver known as Speed. The character Speed only cared about winning races, and, although it made his wife pretty mad, he hardly ever came home. One day, when he and his wife were out for a ride together, there was an argument that ended in a wreck. The wife was killed, and Speed was sorry, but then he went home and found letters that showed she'd been unfaithful all along. After that, of course, there was nothing to stop him from setting out to make every driver in the world eat his dust.

When I'd finished the story I just sat there, playing with a crumb on the white plastic cloth. At first I didn't think at all; then I thought I was going to be sick. Scared of Lester's story? You bet. Right there I saw Speed was the part of Lester I'd sensed the first night driving to the beach, glimpsed an hour or so earlier when Lester was crossing the yards, and met in a hundred ways in the year that lay between those times. No matter what Lester promised, I saw it wasn't any more possible to unite with Speed than to marry the wind.

I put all the stories back in the box and banged the sideboard door shut. Then, still clutching the old dungarees, I went back to the front room and stood uncertainly at the bureau. The mirror was flecked and dusty. How many faces had it reflected? It distorted mine—making the eyes look misty, as if immersed in water. How many faces did a person have? My face was soft in a way some men found beautiful, but it looked boneless—lacking the definition that would have made it memorable. I tried to imagine Lester's face instead of mine—the images overlapping, embracing. But I thought of Walter instead—mouth open, eyes shut.

I dropped the dungarees and opened the left top bureau drawer. Facing me was Lester's large, gold cardboard box of contraceptives. Even when there was little chance of pregnancy, Lester insisted on using those rubbers. When I was still married to Frank I hadn't minded, but since the divorce the thin, yellow condoms had become walls separating me from marriage and the child I hoped to have with Lester.

Snatching up the gold box, I crushed it shut. Then I stuffed it into a paper bag from the kitchen and ran downstairs. With a feeling of relief, I crammed the package into the bottom of a garbage can below orange peels and leftover cereal.

When I returned to the apartment, the phone was ringing. It was

Lester.

"Cynthia—you all right? I got your message but Jack here said you sounded kinda funny when he rang the apartment to—"

"Lester," I blurted, "Walter's dead. Esther stabbed him right here in the street—right in front of our house!"

There was a silence.

"Lester?"

"Un-huh—" His voice was flat, concealing whatever he felt. "She's in for it now," he said finally. "Have the police come?"

"They took her fifteen minutes ago. I tried to call you but nobody answered. I thought you'd want to put it in the paper—"

"Un-huh—" he said again flatly, as if he hadn't heard. "Walter wasn't much," he added slowly with a sigh, but I always kind of liked him." There was another pause, and then Lester returned to his rapid, everyday newspaper voice. "I don't know that we can use the story, Cynthia."

"But why? It was murder in cold blood. I went down to the street. Lester, *I saw the body.*"

"It's a crime of passion, honey. They have those up there every day. I'll tell Jack, but I doubt if he'll want it. The March is what counts."

"You sound as if you don't want to write the story," I said feeling a stab of jealousy. "Was she a friend of yours?"

"Who told you that?"

"Nobody—but when they were dragging her to the police car she shouted something about needing somebody to get her out of jail. I wasn't even sure she was talking to me, Lester, but I got the feeling she meant *you.*"

"Did you answer?"

"No—I didn't get the chance—but when I tried to ask Maria about it afterwards, she ran away."

There was another pause.

"Lester?"

"Yes, honey?"

"Do you know Esther—particularly?"

"Now baby, don't be jealous. You know I know everybody on that block down to the last dog. I knew Esther—maybe even stopped in to talk to her once or twice. Now look, I'm going to get the guy on the police beat to check out your story. Maybe it'll make the paper, but don't count on it. Last night a white guy out in Virginia shot his wife and two kids. We only ran four graphs on *that*. You come on down here after eleven, I've still got civil rights people to call." Before I could answer, he hung up.

I wasn't satisfied, but I knew better than to call Lester back at the paper. It seemed hotter. I went to the window to wait for a breeze. None came. The street was empty with the exception of a few casual passers-by. Cars sped over the spot where Walter had lain. Whatever blood remained was indistinguishable from shadows.

It was only a little before ten, but I was tired. Setting Lester's alarm for ten-thirty, I lay down on my side of the bed. My eyes shut, opened, shut again. Then I went to sleep and dreamed of the March.

In my dream the March was a religious procession instead of a civil rights demonstration. People of all races were struggling down a twisting path to a place—possibly a shrine—I couldn't see.

It got dark, and we were approaching the bottom of a deep, rocky valley. There was a black girl beside me, and I asked her where we were going.

Turning to me, she said quietly: "To the grave—"

Then, with a start, I saw that she looked exactly like me. I was scared, but just then the going got easy. My dark mirror image disappeared, and we were moving effortlessly. Like leaves in a whirlpool, we were all being drawn down to the same place.

Meanwhile there was chanting—a song with a beat like a heart.

Thousands in front of me where singing it. Thousands behind me were singing it. Then below us I saw an enormous face that was neither male or female, black or white. Huge, smiling, indefinite, it was equally comforting and frightening.

And suddenly the line moved faster, the song got louder. I was carried forward, sucked forward, whirled forward—into the shadow-filled mouth of the every-colored androgynous face.

I woke up. The alarm clock was ringing. I shut it off and sat up feeling hung over with sleep and uncomfortably warm.

I walked to the kitchen. Sleazy dotted Swiss curtains drooped at the window. Heat had invaded the apartment, pressing against me like an unpleasant body. In the bathroom, I washed my face with cold water and tried to remember my dream. Like a fish sliding between my hands, it escaped me. I could recall only shadows, the tentative vision of a huge mouth.

I dreamed of death, I thought uncomfortably. Then, brushing my teeth, I forgot I'd dreamed at all.

I dressed and went out. When I got down to the street, I decided not to hail a taxi. Trying not to look at the place where Walter had lain, I hurried toward Fourteenth Street. I would save money by taking the bus. Outsiders might consider the half-block walk unsafe, but in Lester's neighborhood, I reasoned, no harm would come to me.

I passed the quiet fire house. I passed a small group of men lounging on somebody's stoop and scarcely drew a glance. Then I came to the brick house that had freshly painted blinds. Framed in the three-sided bay in front, Edmund Williams was sitting by the middle window reading a book.

When he saw me, he stood up, motioned me to stop. Then Edmund Williams came to the door and said his brother was just going down to the Peoples for a pack of cigarette—so why didn't I wait?

Naturally I did wait, and while he went in to call the much-younger brother he and his wife were putting through law school, I wondered whether he was afraid for me or just being courteous. At the same time, I wanted to know whether he was marching, but— even though Lester and I had been to their house for dinner the winter before—I didn't quite dare ask him.

The dinner, I remembered, was after Lester had written a Civil Service story that mentioned how Edmund Williams, after waiting out years in the lower grades, had finally persevered his way up and been made head of his department—the first black to hold the post.

The story didn't say so, but it turned out that Edmund Williams' father, who'd left him the house, had served forty years as a janitor in the same building where his son now worked. Another thing I'd learned that evening was that Edmund Williams had a gun collection and was a crack marksman who'd been decorated in Korea. His wife, I found out too, was an X-ray technician at D.C. General Hospital.

There were no children—perhaps as a sacrifice to their sober determination to prosper—but the younger brother had lived with them for years like a son.

The front door opened wide and the brother came out. Behind him, I saw Edmund Williams with something in his hand. It was a gun, and for just a moment I thought he was arming himself for what the March might turn out to be. Then I realized it was a piece from his collection which he was polishing with the white cloth he had in his other hand. Raising the weapon benevolently, Edmund Williams nodded and then smiled, and the brother and I went down the block together.

I was embarrassed because I couldn't remember the brother's first name, but it didn't matter. He walked me all the way to the bus stop telling about how he was going to be criminal lawyer. Edmund Williams had just won a medal somewhere for marksmanship, he said, and was slated for another promotion at work.

Right after we said goodbye, a big, brightly lighted, air conditioned bus came and I got on. That was always the way, I decided as I paid my fare and sat down. The things people warned you against—walking down a dark street alone—were seldom a threat. It was the things you did not expect, that no one could have foretold, that were to be feared.

Fourteenth Street was quiet, I saw. No gay, jostling throngs or big cars zooming from one nightclub to another. The flashing red-yellow-blue-lavender neon signs illuminated empty sidewalks. The marquee of one movie house was already dark.

Downtown, I got off, walked the short blocks to the paper and rode an empty elevator to the fifth floor. When I visited Lester in the daytime, I felt out of place—and intruder. In the evening it was different. Reporters who were too busy to say hello at four were at ease at their desks after the first edition unless it was one of the rare times a big story was breaking late.

That night could have been hectic with the March the next day, but as I walked between the long rows of desks, I sensed nothing was happening. Only a few typewriters were clattering. At the night city editor's desk, Jack was leaning back smoking a cigar. Many reporters' places were empty.

I was all set to tell Lester everything about the murder, but of course he was on the phone when I got to him. "I couldn't get much of a night before the March story," he whispered, handing me his pink carbon sheets.

"With the largest civil rights demonstration in Washington history scheduled for this morning," I read, "the city remained quiet last night.

"Bars and cafes reported less-than-normal business...."

"A police spokesman said there was 'no unusual activity' in the streets....

"A local Civil Rights leader predicted that the March by an estimated two hundred thousand persons would be an entirely peaceful demonstration…."

"Look what just came in over the wires," Lester said, handing me a teletype story as he hung up the phone.

Setting down the story he had written, I read:

HITCH HIKER ATTACKED

JOPPA, MARYLAND—

A GRADUATE STUDENT FROM NEW YORK UNIVERSITY WAS ATTACKED ABOUT SIX P.M. BY A MOTORIST WHO HAD STOPPED AND OFFERED HIM A RIDE ON ROUTE ONE.

THE HITCHHIKER, ARTHUR W. ALLEN, JR., 25, OF MANHATTAN, WAS ON HIS WAY TO THE MARCH ON WASHINGTON. ALLEN, A NEGRO, SAID HE HAD A DISAGREEMENT WITH THE UNIDENTIFIED WHITE MOTORIST WHO…."

"Where's Joppa?" I demanded.

"North of Baltimore." Lester didn't bother to give me the rest of the story; he just laid it down on his desk and put his hand on it. "You know what I think?"

I nodded, our eyes met. "It was Billy?"

"More than likely—"

"What are you going to do?"

"Print it tomorrow," he said, louder than he had to.

"But I thought I'd at least tell Bill tonight and see if—"

He was interrupted by a long distance call. "Walter's murder made the paper after all," he told me quickly as he waited for the operator to put the person through. "The Police reporter checked it out and did a couple of graphs.

Walter wasn't her husband, you know."

"Maria said he was."

"If he was, he commuted. She had other guys. I never saw him at her house much."

"At her house? What were you doing at her house?"

Lester gave me a look that made me feel cold. Then his call came through. "Go down and get some coffee," he told me quickly. "I won't be long."

I turned away, walked around past the cable desk to the back elevator. He slept with her, I thought, and immediately disliked myself. Looking back, I saw him hang up the phone and turn to the typewriter again, his face pale and tired under the fluorescent lights. I loved him. If he had been in Esther's apartment, I told myself quickly, firmly blocking the other thought, it was surely on some story.

The elevator was slow in coming. I turned my attention from Lester to the city room itself, looking past the teletype machines to the horseshoe-shaped table where rewrite men sat behind the row of editors' desks. Along the far wall was a row of glassed-in offices for important editors and certain columnists. In several cubicles, lights still burned. On floors above, clerical people from the accounting department and administrative offices arrived at nine and left at five. On floors below, blue-shirted pressmen sweated through the night to print the morning editions. But in the city room there were people working no matter what time it was. It was the hub—the place where events were channeled as quickly as they happened, recorded, sent out, set aside to make way for even more recent news.

In the spring after my divorce, Lester had suggested I come to work for the paper. "You could start as a secretary or even answering the phone," he'd told me. "You'd like it once you got into it. You'd be a good reporter if you got down to business and stopped dreaming."

"Maybe…." I'd been afraid, uncertain—as on the beach when I couldn't plunge into the sea.

But at that moment—with the sound of the news coming in over the teletypes, the editors calling to the reporters, the telephones ringing—the newspaper beckoned like life itself. To me, one murder was the event of a lifetime. To Lester and the other reporters, it was a daily occurrence. As the huge elevator came and I got on, I told myself that I wasn't going to question Lester about Esther again. Even if he knew her well, what did it matter? It was part of his job.

Like the offices, the small company cafeteria was painted grey. No frills at the paper—reality plan and unvarnished and, in the end, reassuring. After I'd bought a cup of coffee and seated myself at one of the small, plastic-topped tables, Melvin Anderson came in and joined me. No older than I was, he was one of the paper's two black reporters— the impressive product of a long rise from Mississippi cotton fields. I'd only met him a couple times, but I knew he was one of the people Lester admired most.

"Haven't seen you all summer," Melvin said. "Have you been letting Lester be lonely?"

I smiled, feeling uncomfortable but trying to think of a polite answer. I admired Melvin, not only because Lester did, but because his struggles far surpassed anything I'd experience in the minor tribulations of my thirty years. Yet, even innocuous questions about Lester embarrassed me. Increasingly, I was ashamed of being a girlfriend rather than a wife—not for moral reasons but because it made me feel unimportant—a "second class" woman.

Without waiting for me to answer, Melvin began talking about the March. I sensed he'd been thinking about it for weeks. His eyes shone; his voice, though quiet, was full of feeling.

"It began as a tribute to Medgar Evers," Melvin was saying. "Then it outgrew that. It became a tribute to everybody from Frederick

Douglass to A. Philip Randolph to some kid born last night."

"This isn't the first march Randolph's led," he added after a moment. "It wasn't enough for *him* just to be president of the Sleeping Car Porters. Way back in 1941 he made his first march on Washington and forced F.D.R. to set up the Fair Employment Practices Commission and put blacks in war industry. In 1948 Randolph was back again telling Harry Truman we weren't going to register for the draft unless he integrated the armed forces. In 1955 when the AFL-CIO merged, Randolph forced them to outlaw racial discrimination. In 1957 on the third anniversary of the Supreme Court school decision, he was back here with twenty thousand people asking Ike to speak out for civil rights. In 1960 they made him president of the Negro American Labor Council." Melvin paused for breath, drawing his chair closer to the table.

"Randolph's big," he went on almost immediately, "but he's only one of them. In 1960 four kids from North Carolina Agricultural and Technical College walked into Woolworth's in Greensboro and sat at the all-white lunch counter. In the next seven months, *seventy thousand* people participated in sit-ins all over the South and as far away as Illinois and Nevada. And long before that in Montgomery, Martin Luther King had—but you know all this—you write history books—" Melvin finished his coffee in a gulp.

It took me a moment to come back to myself and answer. "I didn't know a lot of it," I told him finally. "I'm only a researcher—not a writer." I didn't tell him that certain people at work had often suggested a black heroes history book—only to have the idea vetoed by others. Usually I waited at my desk for what work came, but the next time, I told myself, I'd stand up for that book.

Melvin set his cup back into its saucer. "Would you believe it—" he began in a more conversational tone, "a friend of mine just got himself roughed up by some dumb cracker up in Maryland?" He paused, shoved the saucer aside. "In a way it's ironic—he's sort of an idealist—you know—nonviolent—getting a degree in philosophy in New York."

Still thinking about the March, I was only half listening. For the first time, I felt glad instead of queasy because I was going. If so many others had stood up to fear—

"—he came by here about an hour ago to get the key for my place so he can stay over and march tomorrow," Melvin was saying, "but would you believe it—he was hardly even mad—"

"Why?" I demanded, trying to pay attention.

"Said that the white guy who'd bothered him was heading for Washington, and that what was going to happen here tomorrow would just *show* him." Melvin sighed, shifted, put the cover on the sugar bowl. "Of course, he should have known better than to hitch a ride," he paused, "—especially with a Southerner—"

An unpleasant thought rose in my mind, but I didn't let it surface.

"I suppose the police won't catch the guy, but even if they do— I'm not so sure I could get Arthur to testify—"

The name clicked. I was immediately and unhappily certain that Melvin's friend was the Arthur of Lester's teletype story.

"—and it's insane, I suppose," Melvin was saying, "but maybe Arthur's got the right idea. I mean if everybody—"

"Yes," I heard myself echoing, the words coming like a cork from a bottle,"—if everybody—"

Before I could decide whether to tell Melvin about the teletype story, he was back to the March again.

"—of course New Yorkers like Arthur," he told me, "—they're just a drop in the bucket. People are coming from Massachusetts; they're coming from California. They're coming from Carolina, Georgia, Mississippi, Ohio. Tomorrow morning there'll be tens of thousand," he paused, giving himself to the dream, "—black people, white people—

all of us."

Melvin leaned forward, the warmth of his breath struck my cheek. Under the table, his knee brushed mine. "All of us together," he reiterated softly. His fingers grazed my arm, lingering for a moment on a small, brown sun spot.

The light touch startled me, but I understood. Part of me is the same color as he is, I thought, part of me—

I saw Lester looming up behind Melvin like a thunder cloud. "Come on, honey," he said, grabbing my arm roughly. "Let's get out of here."

Before I could even say good-bye to Melvin, Lester dragged me away.

"What's wrong?" I demanded in the hall.

Lester banged the elevator buzzer and glared at me. "When I came in you were letting that nigger touch you. I *saw* you!"

I stared at him amazed. If he hadn't been so furious, I would have laughed. Instead, I tried to explain. "He *wasn't*" I said, "he was telling me about the March. It was wonderful what he said. Besides, Melvin is one of your best friends. How can you call him a —-?" I couldn't bring myself to say the word.

"If he touches my girl, he's a nigger," Lester said.

The elevator door opened with a thud and we went down.

"His hand grazed my arm—that was all. We were having *coffee*." I knew that it was impossible to explain the symbolism of the gesture, let alone tell him about Arthur. "You're still a stupid Southerner even if you call yourself a liberal," I told him.

We walked out of the building and turned toward Fifteenth Street. It was cooler. A light breeze had sprung up.

"I'm sorry," Lester said very softly after we'd gone half a block in silence. He circled my neck with a comforting arm and kissed me.

The miserable tension faded. He'd been unjust, but I couldn't stay angry. Since I'd learned jealousy the same way he had, I had sympathy. If Lester was unreasonably jealous and suspicious—well—maybe I was too.

We had to wait at the corner for the light to change, and I stood close, holding his arm. "You like the Georgia Lounge, don't you?" Lester demanded in a way that showed he knew I'd forgiven him. Grinning, he chucked me under the chin. "I bet old Bill's over there having a cool one right now," he added. "He doesn't touch a drop at home, but when he gets away from his wife he catches up with himself pretty quick."

We both laughed a little, but then I started thinking about what Melvin had said. First I hesitated, but then I couldn't hold it in any more—I told Lester the whole thing.

We were in the middle of the street when I finished, but Lester stopped dead. "You mean that Melvin's friend Arthur is the hitchhiker that Billy—" he broke off. "Oh gee," he burst out finally, "oh *gee*—"

We stood there for maybe half a minute—occasional midnight cars whooshing by us over the warm pavement. Then Lester straightened; his face got hard. "If Bill's the one that did it, he's going to have to face up to it. Might as well be now as later." Quickly, Lester led me to the sidewalk, and in a moment he was opening the glass door under the red and green neon sign that had a clock in the center and said "GEORGIA LOUNGE."

The Lounge was a newspaper hangout. They cashed paychecks on Fridays, and Mary the owner-waitress had known generations of copy boys and seen big editors come and go.

Lester led me in past the white-capped pressmen who always thronged the bar at midnight when pages were being revised between runs. We headed back toward the double row of booths upholstered in white plastic. Lester waved at Mary, who was serving drinks to some reporters; then he spotted Billy in a back booth finishing a beer. "Bill, you old horse thief!"

"Les!" Billy rose, his red face beaming. Somehow I'd expected Billy to be little and mean, but of course he was big. As he clasped Lester's hand a tiny tear crept down the crease of his plump cheek.

Billy was Lester's age but fifty pounds heavier, and it aged him. His soft, sandy-colored hair had receded a little, adding an inch or two to his forehead. He was wearing a dark brown suit and a tan sport shirt open at the neck. Instead of a tie, he had a thin black cord that dangled loosely from a sliding silver clasp.

"Sure pleased to meet you, Cynthia," Billy said when Lester introduced us. "Does he give you much trouble?" he demanded good-naturedly, jerking his thumb at Lester.

Lester laughed. We sat down, and Lester said something about having the same kind of beer Billy had been drinking, but Billy wouldn't hear of it. He was really going to buy us champagne. Billy had been the host at the fabled New Year's Eve party that had made Lester decide to give up hard liquor. "We were tighter than a couple of flop house ticks that night," Billy recalled with a chuckle. "I've seen deacons back home make resolutions the morning after," he told me, "but they never stuck but a month or so. Takes Lester to keep his five years, I guess, strength of a *mule*—"

We all laughed, Mary came to take the order, and for an instant I wondered whether if it was possible to resolve away a part of one's self.

Then, after Billy had ordered, there was a little silence because Lester was trying to work himself up to the subject of Arthur, and I was feeling uncomfortable because of what Lester had said to Billy about me on the phone back in the apartment.

Billy didn't quite get it, but maybe because he sensed trouble coming between him and Lester, he began talking to me. I was hesitant, but he was open. Even before the champagne came, he'd gotten me talking about how my parents had retired from suburban New Jersey to Southern California and found out that both of us had been raised as Methodists. When I saw Billy wasn't the sort to judge somebody, I relaxed. In contrast to Lester, Billy was big and slow, but like Lester he was warm—needing to draw people to him.

Our first toast was to Billy's wife Estelle and the baby born in April; then we drank to the other three daughters in turn. After that Billy took a pink leatherette folder from his inside coat pocket and showed us snapshots. The oldest was a ten-year-old with corkscrew curls, but the three little ones had all been photographed soon after birth on the same, lace-trimmed pillow. If Billy was sorry they weren't boys, he didn't act it. Each infant was shown happily naked—seemingly flashing her sex like a diamond.

As Billy boasted about the oldest, "—top of her class and going to be a real looker too—" I remembered Lester had told me she wasn't Billy's at all but the product of a teenage affair between his French wife, before he'd met her, and an American soldier on leave in Paris. It didn't seem to matter. A big man, a warm man, Billy had more than enough love for all. I saw why Lester was partial to Billy.

Billy laughed. Champagne flowed down to scatter foam pearls on his ample belly bulge. The more he drank, the more his flesh seemed to fill with the juice of love. "—and I guess we've got another on the way already—" Billy announced Estelle's latest pregnancy with obvious pride as he again drained his glass.

"Gosh Bill, didn't I ever tell you about the drugstore?" Lester bantered, but Billy only laughed again. With a generous, loose-fingered hand, Billy beckoned for more champagne to be brought to our table.

Billy started the second bottle by toasting me. Then he told Lester how he was glad to see he'd finally found himself a good woman. I was pleased by that simple compliment, but I was worried. It seemed impossible that Billy could have attacked Arthur the pacifist. Was it a coincidence? I was waiting for Lester to set the matter straight.

Instead, Lester was looking worse by the minute. He had emptied his first glass in a few swallows, but he just hunched himself over the second without drinking, turning the bowl of goblet between his palms and then staring into it as if there were a hair coiled in the bottom or something worse. He looked like a man hesitating to plunge his hand to the bottom of a dark place.

I wouldn't have expected Billy to notice it in the midst of what he was saying about home and family (his father, a preacher, had received a call to West Texas), but he sensed it. Draining his glass and pouring more, he shut the leatherette picture folder he'd been showing us. "You know, Les," he said in a way that suggested it was the thing we'd been discussing all along, "most everybody I know at home's real worried—I mean, how are things going to *be* when my girls get big? It's hard to *believe* how some of these niggers now will do you if you give them half the chance. Now take today for instance—"

Lester looked up, and seeing he had his friend's attention, Billy paused. With a fat man's exaggerated delicacy, he took small sips of champagne with his little finger extended.

I began to wonder if Billy wasn't smarter than I'd thought and whether some of what he'd been saying hadn't been to soften Lester for what he was about to tell. With the acuity of an animal, Billy appeared to be leading rather than just evading us.

But before Billy got started, Lester interrupted. "Bill," he demanded in a cat's paw voice, "this hitchhiker you said on the phone you had a fight with—was he black?"

Billy straightened suddenly, took a handful of peanuts from the plastic dish beside the ashtray and chuckled a little as he chewed. "Why sure he was a nigger, Les—it wouldn't have *happened* otherwise—"

"You were in Joppa, Maryland?"

"Hell Les, I don't know the name of where I was—I was maybe fifteen miles north of Baltimore coming down from New Jersey—" The champagne seemed to be oozing through Billy's skin; I saw beads of moisture on his forehead. He was not as red as he had been, I noticed, but his voice was louder than before.

"That says it." Lester emptied the glass he had been holding for so long and pushed it aside instead of holding it out for more.

"How do you mean, friend?" Billy demanded belligerently, resting the heels of his hands on the table's edge and leaning forward.

"The guy you hit," Lester told him, "it turns out he was a good friend of a friend of mine."

"A *white* guy?" For the first time, Billy seemed genuinely concerned.

"Black."

"Oh well—" Billy waved a large hand, the palm moist from his glass. "We don't have to worry then, do we?" He smiled broadly, but I sensed there was fear behind it. He was waiting to see the tack Lester would take.

"The friend," Lester told him slowly, "is the best civil rights reporter the paper's got."

I expected that would make Billy cave in, but he only shifted, leaned back and rested his head against the booth's padded plastic. "I needn't ask then," he said with his eyes half shut, "if there's going to be a story about it. I mean, you wouldn't have known it was a place called Joppa if there hadn't been something come in about me."

"There'll be something in the paper tomorrow," Lester told him, "But not because of my friend Melvin. Fact is, I don't think he's even read the story. *I* put it there."

Billy blinked, blanched. "But that could be all right, Les," he said with a pleading note in his voice, "—I mean, as long as they didn't get my license number—?"

"Look—" Lester said in a way that made me think of a hand shutting a door.

"No, *you* look," Billy told him with renewed bluster. "I don't know what your fool story says," he went on righteously, "but it happened like this—I would have given you the whole thing earlier but that Baltimore filling station I called you from was just *dancing* with darkies. I wouldn't be surprised if they weren't running a crap game in back—or something worse." Billy smiled. "There was this little yellow gal there that sure looked like she'd—" Billy glanced at me, broke off, daubed the corners of his mouth lightly with a wrinkled white handkerchief. "Look, I was driving through this town—Joppa, you say it was, when I saw a nigger standing at the side of the road. I figured he was going the way I was, so I stopped and he hopped in—all thank you-sir and humble pie. I was all set to pull out again, when what do you think? The prettiest little blondie you ever saw—if she was a day over seventeen she didn't show it—come up to the far side of the car from somewhere and says was I going to Washington and can she ride. Before I could say a thing she had the door open—or maybe the nigger helped her—for all I know they could have been in cahoots from the start—and right away there they were—both of them—in my front seat and haunch to haunch, snug as chickens in a barn."

"Well Les, it didn't take me long to tell them I wasn't taking a white gal for a ride with no nigger, and the little girl—she sort of screeched a little, but she hopped out quick. But that boy, Lester, he sure was the *dumbest* nigger—I mean he just *sat* there staring at me with those big funny eyes they have. I'd swear he was taller than I was, Les, but you'd of thought he was an itty bitty black rabbit and I was a great big snake—it was as though he was *hypnotized* or something. By that time I was pretty mad, so since he didn't seem ready to go by himself, I gave him a good shove and maybe hit him a couple of times to teach him some manners. The funny thing was, Les, even then—he didn't raise his hand or anything. He just sort of slid off the seat like cold molasses. Soon as he was out, I slammed the door and pulled out quick. But I got a little glimpse of him in the back mirror, and he hadn't bothered to pick himself up yet. Afterwards I got to worrying a little about it, so I called you up. Folks are funny about niggers up here—I mean they treat them like they was made of *glass* or something."

"Billy," Lester said, leaning back against the upholstery of the booth with a funny sort of smile, "you always were a damn fool."

I expected Billy to get angry, but instead he smiled, shrugged, bridled. "I expect you're right, Les," he said ingratiatingly, grinning at us both over his empty glass.

"That guy is a pacifist getting his Ph.D. at New York University— that's how come he never hit you back." Lester paused, "—or maybe he'd forgotten how—"

"Aw now Les—" Billy began blandly.

"But you needn't worry," Lester cut in, "because as far as I saw from what came in over the wires tonight *nobody* got your license number. You can go home and forget it—if you can *live* with it—"

"But Les—come on—" For the first time, Billy seemed genuinely troubled. He leaned forward, his hand rested for a moment on Lester's sleeve. It was not the incident that bothered him, I saw, but Lester's displeasure.

There was a silence. Hunched over the table top, Billy was tracing rings of moisture on the dark red plastic surface. For the second time that night, I saw how weary Lester looked. There was a drained expression on his face.

"O.K. Les," Billy said finally, looking up, "—you want me to go and turn myself in?"

"Oh hell, Bill," Lester said quickly, "the police have got enough on their hands now without *you*. Why don't you go over to where this Arthur is and make it right with the guy—offer to cover his doctor's bill—*do* something. I'll give you the address, but you'd better go over tonight, even if you have to wake him—he'll be gone tomorrow morning."

For the first time in a number of minutes, Billy smiled. The point of his tongue slipped out at the corner of his mouth and ran between his lips. For an instant I thought I saw the catch-me-if-you-can look of a boy getting away with something, but his voice belied it. "Well all right, Les," he said sonorously in a preacher's tones, "I guess I'll just *do* that." He paused, poured out the last of the second bottle of champagne, "Do you think twenty's enough?" He allowed himself a generous sip.

"Nothing's enough—just act like he's *human*—"

"Damn it, Les, I don't like that—did you forget how I save Aunt Annabel?"

I had to excuse myself to go to the ladies room just then, so I didn't hear the end of what Billy was saying. I was almost sure though, that Lester had told me how Billy, at considerable risk to himself, had succeeded in rescuing an old black woman called Annabel from her shack when there was a flood. Unfortunately the woman had died of pneumonia afterwards, and some had suggested burying her in the cemetery near her home. But then—Lester had used it as an example of the way things were where he came from—Billy had been among the first to say that the place was only for whites. It wasn't long before the opposition crumbled, and Aunt Annabel was laid to rest twenty miles away in the all-black graveyard down by the river.

When I left the ladies' room, I noticed a new bottle of champagne on the table. Billy was leaning forward over a full glass, saying something to Lester in a low voice.

"—been hankering to get me a little dark meat, Les," I overheard as I approached the booth. "A guy back at my hotel was telling me there was places here you couldn't go but a block without all sorts of nigger gals coming up and asking you to—"

"You'd be smart to stay away from places like that," I heard Lester tell him. "Only last week over there they took some poor boob from the suburbs back into an alley and beat him so bad he died a couple of days later in the hospital."

Lester caught sight of me, flushed, and then rose quickly so I could slide into my pace.

"I can take care of myself, Les," Billy said with a look I didn't like.

"Sure," Lester shot back, "but even the careful guys that lock their wallets in the glove compartments come back and find somebody broke into their cars."

The conversation died. I knew what Billy wanted, but I could see he wasn't going to outright admit it in front of me. Immediately, I liked Billy less. No longer warm and generous, his fat seemed blubbery. He was shrinking into a moist bag of flesh.

Reading my mood, Lester tried to change the subject. "Last summer when Billy was up here he stayed over in my apartment," Lester reminded me. "Sunday morning I drove him around to the sights, and that afternoon we went out to Arlington Cemetery to see where Bud is. That's the last time I've been there," he went on slowly,"—'cept for when I went with you—"

I thought of the white markers and rolling expanses of the enormous military burying ground and of how Lester, on one of my first weekends in Washington, had taken me to see the grave of Bud, a college classmate. Bud and Lester had both enlisted in the Air Force the day after graduation. Only a year later, Bud had crashed unexpectedly on a flight from Omaha where they were stationed.

The sadness Lester had made me feel then came back, but along with it I was still angry, maybe at Billy, maybe at myself. Why should what Billy wanted bother me, I wondered, when I'd sat through the whole story of Arthur calmly, almost as if it were imaginary? Immediately I knew why. The answer was Frank. What Billy had done to Arthur was remote, grotesque, but what he was going to do to his wife had been done to me.

"Say, Les—" Billy said thickly, draining his glass and then burping comfortably. "Do you remember that Sunday night when I was here the other time?" He paused to wipe globules of champagne from his lips with the back of his hand. "Whatever happened to that big old gal that we—"

"Oh—" Billy jumped as though Lester had kicked him under the table. "Well, excuse me folks—" he rose and shuffled off to the men's room.

"What did Billy mean about last summer?" I demanded as soon as he was gone.

"Cynthia—" Lester's hand lingered comfortingly on my shoulder; "I guess I don't have to tell you Billy isn't one of the brightest guys in the world." He paused. "Could be Bill was only talking to hear his head rattle—" he essayed softly. Then seemingly untroubled by my immediate flash of disbelief, he added: "but it's a mite unlikely—isn't it?" His eyes engaged mine.

"You told me Billy used to play around—" I said stiffly and then stopped, powerless to probe further.

"Only when he's away from home on trips, hon," Lester countered gently. "He plays hell with some bar girl for a night or so— then it's all over."

"You said Billy got VD—"

"That's right. Fact is he's had it so many times that a couple years ago a doctor told him they maybe couldn't give him penicillin any more—he was getting allergic or something. That sent him home primed with repentance, but it wasn't a year but he'd go the itch again and—" Lester paused.

I felt he was keeping something from me out of love, and I didn't know whether to be angry or grateful. His hand left my shoulder; I sensed he was reliving a scene in which I had no part.

"And that woman from last summer that Billy said—?" I asked.

"He was horsing around with somebody from my block all right." Lester shifted as if to shake off a troubling dream. "But it was one of those weeks I was working nights at the paper. I had Sunday off, so that was the only time we—"

"Where was *I*?"

"In New York, honey. Don't you remember how you came down afterwards? It was your first weekend in Washington, and you threw out all the empty beer cans Billy'd left behind."

I nodded. The facts fitted, but I couldn't help wondering if there wasn't more to it. Not that Lester lied—don't believe it. But truthfully, there were some differences between things that happened and the stories his heart said needed to be told. The grayness of what was over and past got colored with the urgency of now and here. Of course where I worked they did the same thing. Afterwards though, they called it history.

"Here he comes," Lester warned, watching Billy chart a broad and wavering course to the booth. "I've had my fill, but I don't believe we can get shut of him till we finish the bottle. Bill isn't rich, you know—just because he's buying us champagne. He doesn't even earn what I do—and with all those kids—I wouldn't be surprised if he's been pinching pennies for a month just so he could show me a good time—"

When Billy came back he seemed happy, even a little light-headed, like a boy let out of school. He poured us more champagne and had sandwiches brought, and briefly we saw again the warm, generous host of the first bottle. But then—it wasn't anything direct—just little asides—it got pretty clear Billy wanted to make Lester tell him about some black woman who would take him on.

And it even got so Lester was joshing him about it—playing with him, cat and mouse. But at the same time it seemed only part of Lester was leading Billy on—the rest of him holding back, marking

68

time. Finally though, Lester got carried away with his own bandying. Holding out his glass and letting Billy fill it till foam sloshed over the sides, Lester jibed: "—and do you recollect the one I told you last summer about the segregationist mayor who came up north here for a convention?"

"Yeah?" Billy obviously didn't remember.

"He was from Alabama," Lester began, "and the first night he hit town he—" Lester hesitated, glanced quickly at me, sipped champagne.

Right away, I knew what was wrong. Lester, like Billy, hesitated to discuss certain things in front of a woman, no matter how well he knew her. The idea made me angry—whether at myself or Lester I wasn't sure. I had the feeling I wasn't going to like the story, but at the same time I was determined to hear it through. Quickly, as though kicking a stone from a path, I begged Lester to go on.

Lester looked at me, then Billy, but still he hesitated, twisting the stem of his glass between thumb and forefinger, clearing his throat. I realized there was more bothering him besides what I'd thought; then, maybe because I'd begged him, Lester gave us the whole thing.

"Well this old mayor," Lester began, "it was his first night in Washington. After he had his dinner at The Statler Hotel where he was staying, he hied himself out for a little walk. He hadn't gone but a block or so before a black guy named Racehorse came up and started talking to him. Now Racehorse, it turned out, had a lot of pictures of girls he was carrying in his pocket. And the mayor—he liked some of those black gals pretty well. So when Racehorse told him he wouldn't mind making introductions, that mayor was mighty amenable. Old Racehorse took him up to where there were bars he knew, and they stopped at some place called Cecil's and had some drinks. Then old Racehorse took him around the corner, and—"

"Cecil's?" Billy broke in. "I saw a bar with a name like that on the way in. There was a wreck on Rhode Island Avenue, and I had to detour and drive real slow. This place was on T Street right around Seventh, I'd almost swear to it. Les—?" Billy leaned forward, resting an imploring paw on Lester's arm.

"Now I don't rightly recall the address," Lester said evenly, brushing Billy aside like a fly. Besides, it *might* have been Cecil's, but it might just as well've been some other name. Anyway," he went on quickly, "Racehorse took that mayor around the corner to some apartment house. He told the mayor it was the building where some of those girls lived, and he got the poor sucker to stand in the hallway while he went to get one. Before he left though, he got the old boy to put his wallet in an envelope which they hid behind the hall radiator for safekeeping.

"After Racehorse was gone, the mayor waited a good while. Finally though he got tired, and he went over to the radiator to get his wallet. The envelope was there, all right—but there wasn't a thing in it but a wad of newspaper.

"The mayor saw it was the Murphy game," Lester went on, "and he was pretty made about it. Later that night though, he was even sorrier. Seems there'd been a robbery and stabbing up around there that same night, and pretty soon the police picked up Racehorse on suspicion because they saw he was spending a lot of money in one of those bars. Racehorse hadn't killed anybody, but he didn't like the look of things, so he told them about the mayor right away. Racehorse still had the old boy's wallet with him so it was easy as pie for a detective and a police reporter to take it right over to the Statler.

"Of course they asked the mayor if he'd been looking for black women. And that old mayor—" Lester couldn't help laughing, "he told them, 'Gosh no.' Somehow though," Lester went on with a chuckle, "that didn't go down too well when the wire service story hit the headlines in the guy's home town the next day."

That was end, and we all laughed. Billy laughed the longest.

If Lester had meant the story as a lecture, it had the opposite effect. The incident made sin seem funny, and besides, it had all happened to someone else. Lester applied himself to his glass. I let Billy freshen mine. Champagne bubbles came up inside my nose, and I watched the way the red and blue lights of a revolving beer ad tinted the dusty ceiling.

"Bill—I have to work tomorrow—"Lester said finally, turning his empty glass upside down.

Billy did not seem to mind. When I refused it, he poured out the last of the bottle for himself. He beckoned for the check, and when Mary came to total what we'd had, he joked with her as if she were an old friend.

The champagne had coarsened Billy, I noticed, but it had brightened Lester's magnetism. In spite of his old suit, (Lester was wearing the blue suit I knew he'd bought to be married in five years before) he glowed, he shone. It occurred to me that Lester could outfight and out love any man in the room.

Mary seemed to sense the same thing. While Billy peeled bills from a roll pinched by a silver clip, Mary lingered to talk to Lester, using his name more than once and letting her fingertips rest on his shoulder. When she left, a girl in another booth began looking at Lester. Then after that, a woman in black linked eyes with Lester as she sauntered by.

While we waited what seemed to be a long time for Billy's change, Lester told Billy about how he'd interviewed the President for a civil rights story, and Billy could hardly believe it. "Gee, Les," he demanded, "—I mean—what was he *like*?"

Then the talk slid to other subjects; it was Billy's turn to reminisce. "Say," he demanded, smiling broadly, "do you remember Wilma?"

"Sure I do," Lester told him. "Wilma McCrothers from history class—she was stacked up like something out of this world." He grinned.

"Yeah well-you ought to see her now—"

"How—?"

"Why she's had four kids and taken on so much blubber she's having trouble getting through doors sideways. I ran into her once a couple of weeks back, and I swear, she's grey as a rat."

"That's hard to believe," Lester said. "She used to be a fine looking piece—I mean—" He frowned, reddened, "—I'm sorry, hon."

He slid his arm around my waist, and I smiled, nodded, maybe I even laughed. After all—what was there to say? I had the fleeting image of Wilma as a grey, outdated sedan with bulbous fenders; then Mary came with the change.

Lester buttoned his coat, Billy fed the juke box a final coin. Then, just before we got up, I had a false but uncomfortable feeling that Lester was sitting across the table beside Billy instead of next to me. I had lost him, I felt, and suddenly it was male against female, South against North, two against one. The idea faded, but there was an aftertaste of isolation. Then Lester took my hand, and we went.

We got only as far as the bar, then waited while Billy ducked back to the men's room once more. "Who was Wilma?" I couldn't help asking even though we were standing in an awkward spot where we had to move aside every time a waitress came through.

"Nobody I cared about—" Lester bent towards me, his eyes leveled with mine.

I knew it was true, but at the same time the answer made my stomach ache. "She wasn't the one where they had the tape recorder?"

"Oh no—that was Rhoda—"

Billy was with us again, we turned. He drew Lester forward amicably, and I came behind like the tail of a kite.

My mind clung to the story Lester had once told me of how someone named Rhoda had discovered that her lover, a football star, had been putting a tape recorder under their bed and then playing everything

72

back for his friends. Naturally, I'd wanted to know what she'd done about it. All Lester could tell me though, was that he didn't think Rhoda had seen much of her quarterback after that.

We reached the door; the blast of the big air conditioner above it hit us. Right there is struck me that Rhoda, Wilma and the mayor—and even the dead Aunt Annabel—had one thing in common. Losers. That was why Billy had laughed so about the mayor.

Black or white—what mattered in the South was to win. It wasn't the ethic they preached in churches, but it was harsher, simpler. For the winner applause—for the loser laughter. That way of looking at things (it somehow brought to mind the race car driver in Lester's story) was as natural to Billy as breathing.

Billy opened the door. Warm air hit me like a smothering hand. Abruptly, I wondered when Lester and Billy would be meeting in the Lounge again. And would I be with them then—or left behind like losers in Lester's stories?

Outside on the sidewalk saying good-bye, Billy lingered as if he hated to see the evening end. "Les," he asked finally, "when will I see you?"

"How about tomorrow?" Lester shot back.

Ignoring the invitation to the March, Billy smiled, bridled. His gaze sidled to the street corner where an old peddler was selling corsages from a cardboard panel. "Why say, Miss Cynthia—" he began, ignoring Lester and addressing me playfully, "you'd sure look pretty with one of those—"

Before we could stop him, Billy had peeled a five dollar bill from his roll and bought one. The price was a dollar, but when the old black man said he didn't have change, Billy told him to keep the five. Swaying a little—but at the same time balancing ebulliently on the balls of his feet—Billy returned and presented me with a slightly wilted red carnation.

I had to thank him, but since I saw Lester didn't like it, I made it short.

"Say Bill," Lester cut in before I'd finished, "if you don't quit flashing your wad somebody a lot worse than Racehorse's going to take it away from you for sure."

"If you say so, Les," Billy said with a humility that wasn't very convincing since at the same time he was preening—smoothing his hair, straightening his tie clasp, tucking in his shirt. "I guess I'll just have to remind myself to stay away from Cecil's where old Racehorse took that mayor," he added. "That *was* Seventh and T—wasn't it?" He paused; I was almost sure he winked, but it was too dark to be sure. Then he became serious. "Let's make it for Thursday then," he told Lester quickly—as if they had already settled on the day after the March. "Give me your number so I can call you at work."

I could feel Lester's annoyance, but he didn't let it out. Instead he took one of his business cards and proffered it between two fingers. "You still remember the place I told you where that hitchhiker is?" he demanded. "How about I write it on this?"

"I got it right here, Les." Billy taped his head as though it contained a wealth of knowledge. Then, with surprising agility, he nipped the card from Lester's fingers and inserted it in the breast pocket of his shirt. In the instant before he closed his coat, I saw the small white rectangle gleaming through the thin cloth. Scarcely covering his heart, it seemed but a fragile shield for his massive chest.

"Well, so long then—" Billy turned, waved, and then struck out towards his car—a customized Chevrolet he'd left near Fourteenth Street under a "No Parking" sign. Wavering only slightly, he moved with surprising agility. The darkness slimmed his bulk almost to a shadow, and there was a dapper readiness in his receding figure which I hadn't noticed indoors.

Billy's engine turned over, stalled, finally got going. He gunned it; the sound made me think of stones striking glass.

"Come on, Cynthia—" There was a tiredness in Lester's voice that made me take his hand.

We turned towards Fifteenth Street where Lester had left his car, but I couldn't help looking back. First I saw Billy shoot across Vermont Avenue; then I saw him squeal to a stop for the Fourteenth Street light. The last time I looked, his car—it had a tail light missing—lurched left on Fourteenth instead of turning right towards where Melvin lived. He was on his way to T Street.

For an instant I hated Billy—then I envied him—not for the sex but the knowledge. What was it like, I wondered, to couple casually like an animal and then leave after an hour or a night without knowing the other person's name?

The summer before, Lester and Melvin had worked on a series of articles about prostitution in Washington. Lester had shown me what he'd written, and I'd read about where whores were and what they charged. But how did they feel? What did they think? Such questions were never explored: the editor had decided to kill the series.

We crossed the street. Seeing I knew where Billy had gone, Lester drew me close.

"Will anything happen to him?" I asked unsteadily.

"No, honey, he was in the Marines. He can take care of himself. You don't like it, do you? " Lester released me, sighed. "Well, he kind of skunked me too, didn't he? First hitting on where to go from me just mentioning Cecil's Bar—then the way he was about the March. What in Sam Hill gave me the idea I'd get him to come with us?" Lester shook his head.

"What about the hitchhiker?" I demanded "I mean, do you think Billy will still go over and make it right with Arthur at Melvin's place the way he promised?"

"He'll get there before morning," Lester said, "—not because he wants to, of course, but because he gave me his word."

"Billy's going up to T Street," I began, "it makes me think of the way Frank used to—" Too tired to talk of Frank's infidelities, I broke off. Then, without meaning to, I cried a few champagne tears.

"Aw honey," Lester comforted, "everybody isn't that way. I wouldn't do you like that—"

Before Lester finished, I saw the old peddler crossing the street. Without realizing it, I'd dropped my red carnation.

With a gallant gesture, the black man plucked the flower from the curb and returned it. "Don't you take on, Miss," he admonished authoritatively. Then, apparently believing I was crying because Billy had gone, he added: "I believe he'll be back directly. Not many left like *him*—" he muttered as he shuffled back to his corner. "Generous—" he added in a knell-like whisper, "—a most generous gentleman."

Taking my hand, Lester led me to the car and helped me in. Although I allowed myself to be comforted—blowing my nose on Lester's handkerchief—I disliked myself for descending to the role of wounded woman. Women had to be lied to, Southern men felt, women had to be cozened and coddled. Were they right?

I'd often thought that half of the human race—i.e. women— spent most of their lives pretending life was something it wasn't and acting accordingly. Only through men were realities encountered, I concluded, moving close and letting my head rest on Lester's shoulder. But having met such questions, I wondered dimly (soft, summer night air was flowing through the open windows) where did a woman go?

We were going home. Like a child in a carriage, I had nothing to do but ride. My eyes shut.

When I opened them we were passing the Meridian Hill Park where we sometimes walked—a European-style garden of marble statues, fountains and long perspectives. Trees trailed above us, and as we stopped for a light, I smelled leaves.

"It's a long time since I've been home to Texas," Lester said quietly.

"Do you want to go back?"

"No—maybe—I don't guess so. They're an awful lot of Billy's back home."

"There are?"

"Sure. They're like targets in a shooting gallery—no matter how many times you down 'em, they come up smiling." Lester sighed. "Of course, wasn't but a couple of hours since I called somebody a nigger."

"You were sorry—"

"I was. And like as not if Melvin hadn't been my friend *and* black, I'd've called him worse to his face—maybe even knocked him down.

I nodded and remembered the story of the day after he'd discovered his fiancé's infidelity. That was when Lester had sought out her lover and fought him till he refused to rise. "It wasn't anything with Melvin," I told him.

"I know." We turned right, gliding by the small preserve of grass where Park Road met Sixteenth Street. Then, waiting for the last light at Fourteenth by the Peoples Drug, Lester added: "Sometimes I think that we're just going to have to *die* before even the littlest thing changes. Not just some of us—a whole generation."

"Maybe—" I echoed, not knowing what to say. I thought of all the times at work I'd read about "a generation" at one period of history or another. But how easy it was to generalize when that meant people already gone, and how hard to see that we were no more than the others.

The light changed. We glided past the Tivoli and parked a little beyond the fire house—just a few steps from our front walk. As we got out, I thought of calling Lester's attention to the place Walter had lain. But already the smear looked more like tar than blood, and the murder seemed less than before.

How many died in one day? How many deaths were never even recorded in a newspaper? I dropped Billy's wilted carnation on the tar and stepped on it. Then I followed Lester into the house and up the stairs.

Inside, without turning on the light, we stood together in the front room beside the bed. "—and Cynthia," Lester was saying, "I even worry sometimes because I love you. I want us to be happy—but I'm afraid something will happen." He paused. "We'll always be true, Cynthia—won't we?"

"I'll never be unfaithful to you," I told him, "—never—"

Before I could finish, he engulfed me. Never with Frank had I felt so needed, so desired. I felt that if he could, Lester would have climbed inside my body—not just his penis but all of him.

I was lying on the bed naked and Lester was above me. Reaching behind him, he opened the bureau drawer, fumbled for the contraceptives.

It was only then that I remembered.

"Where are they? He demanded. "They were right here—"

At first I didn't dare answer, then I blurted: "I threw them away—I want to have your baby."

I was half sitting up, my weight resting on my elbows, when he slapped me hard. Light exploded behind my eyes. I was flattened. If I had been standing, he would have knocked me down.

I began to cry. It was the first time he'd ever hit me. I was flattened. It didn't occur to me to try to hit him back.

Instead of being repentant, he was bitter. "Where are they?" he demanded, his face darker than the shadows that packed the room. "Where'd you put them?"

"In the garbage," I gasped. I had never seen him so angry.

In a flash, he had put on his raincoat and his old dungarees, and I heard him running down the stairs. He came up more slowly and switched on the light. He had the battered box in his hand. Almost as if nothing had happened, he set the box on the bureau, undressed and put on one of the rubbers.

I watched him as if he were a freak in the circus performing a repellent feat. Then I turned away, curled into a naked ball in the center of the bed and pulled the sheet over my head.

He snatched away the sheet and approached me roughly, grabbing my breasts, attempting to turn me towards him. I resisted, drew into myself like a turtle and sobbed loudly.

He gave up, turned, sat on the edge of the bed with his back to me, his face in his hands. "Honey," he said when I was quieter, "we can't have a baby, you know that."

"Why not? I'm not married any more."

"Most people wait till they get married again," he said primly over his shoulder, as if lecturing a child.

"Well, we could—couldn't we—anytime?"

"Well—" he hesitated, "I don't know about that. We'll have to see."

"See what?" I demanded in a wail. "Only a few minutes ago you said you loved me."

He turned and faced me. "I do, but honey I don't know whether I'm ready to get married. Maybe I'm still too young."

That brought up a sore point, and I was silent. Since Lester was three years younger, he might even decide not to marry me because I was an "older woman" of thirty. I began to tremble in the way I often had during our first weeks when I was telling him all the cruel things Frank had done to me. My whole body shook.

"Oh honey—" He lay down, taking his usual place beside me,

arranging the sheet around us. "Honey, I'm sorry," he said, stroking the cheek he'd slapped. Maybe it's because of being engaged to Audrey—I suppose I'm still afraid—"

I let him draw me back into his arms, sighed, rested my head on his chest. "Turn off the light," I begged.

The pain was over and I didn't want to talk. What I wanted was to get rid of the fear of losing him—the sinking feeling that he was like Billy or Frank or just wanted a girl friend, a convenience. He loves me, I told myself, knowing it was true. But at the same time, I knew there was a part of Lester I could never hope to hold.

His hands caressed me I the dark room, and slowly, my mind got tired. Then, eager to eradicate questions, I opened myself to him.

When I woke up, the phone was ringing. It was still night, and instinctively, I didn't want Lester to answer it. A crank, I thought sleepily, remembering that one of Frank's girl friends, a nurse, had taken pleasure in ringing my number in the middle of the night before the divorce. Then, waking a little more, I thought of the caller who'd threatened Lester.

Lester picked up the phone. Then there was a silence while the other person talked.

"Yes….Yes, I know him," Lester said in a hoarse, unfamiliar voice. "I'll come."

I switched on the light.

Lester's face was pale and contorted. "Somebody got Billy," he said quickly and turned away from me, his head bent. "He went to get a girl, I guess, and somebody beat him over the head." He drew a long breath. "He died on the way to the hospital."

"Oh, Lester—" I couldn't cry, there was only the sick, empty feeling of shock.

"They want me to come down to the morgue." Lester was already at the closet, putting on his suit.

"I'm coming with you."

Before he could tell me no, I—who was always late to rise—was up and dressing. Billy—big, slow, generous Billy. He didn't deserve to *die*, I thought angrily. With Walter in the street, death had seemed strange, intrusive. Suddenly though, it had become a personal enemy....

"Why did he have to go like *that*?" Lester demanded as he drove through the dark, quiet blocks to the morgue. "It's awful to have to go like that," he went on painfully, "—without so much as a minute to get ready. Even Bud must have known for a little while that his plane wasn't going to make it, but poor old Bill—it sounds as if somebody just snuck up behind him and—" He broke off.

"I ought not to've let him order that third bottle," Lester went on rapidly. "I didn't want it—he didn't need it—but there I was jawing about things like *Wilma*—" Lester spat out the window in self-disgust.

"What about Estelle?" I asked, trying to draw him from his own distress.

"Estelle?" I could see the thought was fresh to him. "I guess I'll have to be the one to call her," he said after a minute. "She's a fine woman, Cynthia, but it's going to be terrible—with all those kids to raise and another one coming."

"Maybe we can do something—maybe we can help her—" My voice trailed off. I didn't go on because I knew I was mouthing platitudes—the empty phrases people always said at such times. There was nothing to do, I realized, and the thought made me feel as if I were standing in front of a big wall of mud.

D.C. General. We turned into the huge hospital complex that contained the morgue. "—the cop that called is a friends of mine," Lester was explaining, "but he only works at headquarters—they hadn't gotten the details. Seems the police found Billy in a parking lot off Seventh Street. His wallet was gone, but my card was still in his shirt. When my friend heard about the card he called the paper, and the operator told him how to get me at home." He paused, squared his shoulders. "Honey, I'm going to have to identify him."

"You mean we have to *look* at him?"

"You won't, honey, but I do. I guess I'm about the only one in town who could tell for sure who he is."

For a moment I felt I couldn't go through with it. To see death twice in one night—everything in me drew back. Yet something else pushed me forward. See, it urged, know, understand.

"He was twenty-seven," Lester said, "—just my age—it could happen to any of us."

Earlier I might have dismissed Lester's words as sentimental. Suddenly, they were real. To any of us, I thought—but not to Lester. Instinctively, I touched his arm, drew closer. The warmth of his flesh reassured me, yet as we rode under the old iron street lamps, I couldn't help noticing how their waxy glimmer shadowed his face, draining his ruddiness to ashes. For an instant, I had the feeling there was something with us in the car. Possibly an enormous quadruped, it seemed to be squatting in the back seat, breathing against our necks....

Of all the buildings, the morgue was the smallest. Set off in a corner beside the farthermost gates, it was a low, red brick box with a small front portico supported by two white columns. Behind, and stretching off to the far side, there was a cemetery.

We parked and got out. Passing a police car standing by the door, we went in. Inside, a pale young interne was waiting for Lester. "I'm very sorry," he said diffidently, introducing himself, shaking Lester's hand. "Your friend never recovered consciousness.

Lester nodded, swallowing hard. I noticed that a large, drowsy policeman was sitting on a scarred wooden bench at the end of the empty waiting room. Clearly he wasn't the friend who'd called Lester, for he didn't come forward. I wondered if he was the one who'd found Billy, and then, looking closer, if he wasn't the one who'd spoken to me in the street beside Walter's body. All policemen look alike, I told myself.

"—if there's anything I can do," the young interne was saying, "you can find me over in the other building—"

Before he could finish, I heard the music. From behind the heavy oak door in the far corner of the room came faint drumbeats augmented by trumpets. The door opened slowly, even the policeman turned to look. A young, light-skinned black man emerged, limping slightly and carrying a small portable radio.

"This is Joe," the interne said, motioning him to tune it down. "He'll take you in."

I'd expected the interne would come with us; instead, he was saying good-bye. Like sea voyagers, we were setting off alone.

Even though it was August, I felt cold. A draft seemed to be flowing towards us from the inner door. Joe beckoned. Lester's hand clutched mine. We followed.

We were in a long, clammy passage without windows. Ahead, his hips and shoulders jerking in a limp that was almost a dance step, Joe moved quickly, a long ring of keys jangling at his side. He had tuned his radio loud again, almost to full volume.

"I've been here to see the coroner on stories," Lester whispered bravely. "Joe's the night man. He remembers me."

The thought started in my mind that Joe was insane. To spend each night in the morgue waiting for bodies…. If Lester hadn't been holding my hand, I would have turned back. The grey-walled corridor had begun to slope gently, and I was afraid that when we got to the bottom we wouldn't be able to rise up again.

We passed brown double doors marked "Inquest Room." We passed a green sign that said: "To the Coroner's Office." At the bend of the corridor Joe paused briefly, adjusting his radio. The music faded—then resumed more quietly.

"Three of them came in this last little while," Joe told us loudly, scratching his neck. "We got to see which gentleman he is." He smiled widely, a wet-lipped, idiot's smile that made me more scared than I was.

Convinced he was crazy, I wanted to say something to Lester. There wasn't time. Joe had already started again, limping off in a loose-hipped way that was almost obscene. We followed.

As the corridor went down, the lights seemed dimmer. We must be under the cemetery, I thought, fantasying that the way would branch into tunnels—underground routes to graves. But instead of branching, the corridor expanded. We were in a grey-walled, low-ceilinged room with six doors.

Quickly, Joe set down the radio and snapped it off. Then, placing a finger on his lips as if her were afraid of awakening someone, he opened one of the doors wide. "Yes sir," he whispered, "I think we found him."

We were standing in a small, refrigerated room that seemed to be lined with filing cabinets—enormous grey steel drawers. Joe bent and tugged on one of the handles. The drawer stuck, then opened heavily. The grey face of an aging white man we didn't know appeared. One look at us told Joe he was the wrong one. "Sorry folks," he said. "Guess we're a little mixed up down here—busy night."

He tugged at another drawer and I caught my breath. It was Walter. No more bubbles rose from his lips, and his mouth was set in a frightening grimace, revealing yellowed teeth.

Joe grinned.

Was it a sadistic game in which he enjoyed disappointing people with the wrong dead? I didn't feel like waiting to find out. "I'll meet you," I whispered to Lester.

Letting myself out as fast as I could, I burst into the outer room with the six doors. The other doors were shut, and suddenly, I realized I'd forgotten which one led to the corridor. My heart pounded unpleasantly, I hesitated. Then I turned left and twisted a heavy brass handle. It was the wrong door.

Before me, three bodies lay on dissecting tables half-dismembered. Two men and one woman. One of the dead men was old, his hair sparse and white, but the other was youngish. His chest cavity had been opened and some of his insides removed to a white enamel dish on a nearby table. His penis lolled limply on his abdomen. Like an arrow, it pointed at the open wound.

I heard a little laugh behind me. "Gotta keep that door shut on account of rats. Come on, little Miss, ain't your time here yet." Joe's hand closed over mine on the handle, drawing the door shut. "Your mister's saying good-bye to his friend. He say tell you he be along shortly."

I drew back. The heavy, cloying odor of the autopsy room had filled my mouth. I was afraid Joe's hand would touch mine again, but instead he went over and got his radio and then opened the door to the corridor—motioning me forward. I didn't want to go with him, but I didn't want to wait alone for Lester either. I started the upward journey.

It was harder than going down. I was numbed by the cold dampness. Every step was an effort, the climb exhausting. Like an enormous gravity, what lay below weighed me down.

Afraid of Joe, I stayed as far behind as I could without losing him. The music on his radio had become slow and mournful. When the corridor turned and I lost sight of him, wailing horns and sighing strings drew me forward.

Finally we came to the place where the corridor leveled. With a surge of strength, I dashed past Joe, left him behind. His music faded. Panting, I came to the great oak door and thrust it open.

I was in the waiting room. The comfortable sounds of summer

welcomed me: the crickets in the grass outside the window, the faint dripping of the water cooler, the soft breathing of the policeman sleeping on the bench while a fly paraded across his forehead. He wasn't the policeman I'd seen on the street, I decided, but a different and perhaps more sympathetic person. I passed without waking him and went outside.

Standing under the portico, I stared at a blank patch of sky between two big trees. Only a few stars and the moon absent, possibly somewhere behind the building. Were the dead up there? I wondered, looking at the sky but at the same time noticing that a small bush was in bloom at the foot of the steps. Or, I wondered fuzzily, was the part of Billy that lay below all there was?

I was feeling better—as if I'd left death behind—so the questions didn't seem too urgent. Relaxing, I leaned against one of the pillars. When Lester finally came out, I was sitting on the top step, sleepily enjoying the night air.

"You saw Billy?" I asked him, getting up quickly.

"Yes." He caught his breath, covered his eyes with his hand.

For a little while we stayed there together, standing close. Then, my arm around his shoulders, I led him to the car.

"You'll drive?" he said finally.

I nodded, and he handed me the keys.

When we were home, we went to the front room and sat on the red couch.

"He was generous," Lester began, "—it wouldn't be stretching it to say he was generous to a fault." Then he went on and told me twice over about how Billy, the son of an impoverished preacher, had helped him with loans Freshman year when Lester's father's cotton crop failed for lack of rain.

"—and he was a good father," Lester added in the manner of a man placing one brick on another. "Do you remember how proud he was of those pictures he had of his kids?"

Trying not to lose track, I nodded sleepily. Then, as Lester went on about other good things Billy's done and I came back with the answers I knew he wanted, it got more believable that the Billy we knew was dead. For our Billy was golden—risen into another person—we had washed him clean with words.

Finally, when he'd said all he could, Lester looked at his watch. "It's getting on towards six," he said, "I suppose I ought to call Estelle."

"*Now?*"

"If I don't' she might have trouble getting on a plane. There aren't that many that run out of there, you know, and I'm certain she'll want to come today." He went to the phone.

After the operator finally put him through to Billy's wife, I realized Lester had been working himself up to that conversation all along. With big tears comings out of his eyes, Lester told Estelle what a wife would have wanted to know. Only a little of "the accident," nothing of Arthur, not even a hint of what Billy'd been doing when he died. It was like hearing the story of the death of a saint.

I suppose that was the way I would have told it too, but somehow, when he hung up, we couldn't look at each other. "What you told her was true," I said finally, my voice trailing off.

"Yes," he said, moving away from the phone, "—but it was only part of it."

We got ready for bed. I hung my dress in the closet. Did the dead live only in what people said about them? I wondered. Then I wondered whether history—which was so often composed of such recollections—wasn't just....

The night was over. Lester snapped of the light. Making his way through the waning darkness, Lester went to the front window and stood, looking out. "What's it like?" he said finally, speaking loudly as if to make himself heard through shadows.

"What?" Already in bed, I raised myself on one elbow.

"Going like that all of a sudden," he answered after a pause, "—Billy—Walter—Bud—how did they *feel*?"

Staring at the indistinct outlines of his body, I wished I could see his face. The question meant a lot to him, I sensed.

"You know what I think," he said finally, turning from the window, "—maybe it's like this—" He went to the corner of the room and squatted beside the ancient television set. Abandoned by a previous tenant, the thing had never really worked, and Lester didn't want to put money into it.

He flipped it on. The screen, as usual, showed only wavy lines. He flipped it off. The equivocal image contracted to a pinpoint of light that faded, leaving the screen empty. "Like that," he said, "—just somebody turning off the lights."

I signed. "Come to bed," I begged. In two hours we would be getting up again.

He came and we lay there, the room a mesh of shadows.

"You still coming to the March?" he asked after a while.

"Yes."

"You're not afraid?"

"Because of tonight, you mean?"

"Well—it was most likely somebody black that—" he broke off. "—that did that to Billy," he finished painfully.

For a moment, the thought ran through my mind that it was the hitchhiker. Then I saw how ridiculous it was to suppose that Melvin's friend Arthur, a pacifist who was undoubtedly sound asleep blocks from where Billy had been, would ever have even wanted to— A black, I told

88

myself, imagining the killer more as a force than a person. Retribution.

"I doubt if the police ever find him either," Lester was saying. "Cases like that—they never seem to catch anybody." He paused tiredly. "If I could just get my hands on him though," he went on with renewed energy, "I'd—"

For some reason—maybe because I was so tired—the idea of the unknown murderer made me think of descending the long, dark corridor in the morgue. I had the feeling of being pulled down, pressed back. Was black a color or a force? I wondered dully.

Then, turning to Lester, I forgot everything else. "Sing me," I begged.

He knew what I wanted. The little Southern lullaby he'd comforted me with so many nights. So he sang in a tired baritone:

"Go to sleepy little baby,

Go to sleepy little baby,

And when you wake

On a patty-patty cake

You'll ride a bright and shining pony."

The song made me feel better. Briefly, I imagined a dazzling horse with stars on his reins. Instead of a Texas cow pony, the horse was a circus charger. Manageable but spirited, the horse cantered comfortably though clouds until he was absorbed in the brilliant, every-colored warmth of an imaginary sun.

The Day

Lester's alarm went off at eight. We slept close, reaching for each other in the night when we lost touch, so his face was only a few inches from mine. Almost immediately, I saw the soft expression of sleep harden with the thought of Billy's death.

"Oh hon—" he buried his head in my shoulder.

I kissed his neck, his hand groped for mine. We lay there for a little while, then he slipped away and I heard water running in the bathroom.

Without him, my strength waned. I shut my eyes and gave in to fantasy—Billy had never come to Washington—the March was far in the future—Lester had the day free and we were going to spend it talking, reading, making love.

Then I remembered that I had been dreaming about Frank. Trying to escape him, I'd forced my body through a broken window. My skin was cut away in patches, and the flesh at those places was dark—almost black.

I got up, took off my nightgown and stood facing the mirror. I was surprised to see my face and body unchanged. Two deaths the day before—and now—? The thought of the March made me feel cold. Quickly, I put on underwear and went to the closet. I chose the most mournful dress I had—brown linen. Then I went to the window and looked down at the place where Walter had been lying.

The street was flooded with sunlight, but something else seemed to linger. I pictured it as a gargoyle crouched on a rooftop, shadowing the street. The gargoyle, I imagined wildly, was a jackal with vulture's wings.

Lester came out of the bathroom, and then I took my turn. After that I went to the kitchen and fixed wheat cakes, Lester's favorite breakfast.

He came right away when I called him, but he didn't eat. Just the way he sat—leaning forward with his head hanging low—showed how he felt. At the same time though, (he was neatly dressed with a clean shirt, his shoes polished) I sensed a certain readiness about him. One part of him was truly mournful, I saw as I drank my orange juice, but another part was alive, active—and indifferent.

Then, thinking of his short story about the race car driver whose only aim was to win, I wondered how much Lester cared about Billy— or anyone. No, it wasn't that Lester lacked feeling, I decided, but that he lived in the present. And Billy, because he was dead, was *past*.

Lester poured syrup over his wheat cakes, but he only picked at them. "Billy was the best friend I ever had," he said finally, pushing his plate aside.

I nodded, wondering if it was so. Lester had so many friends— did Billy's loss make him seem most precious? Still, like other things Lester said, it sounded true and moving—whereas fact would have rung flat. Only by hyperbole, I decided, could a Southerner lay another Southerner to rest.

"—or maybe my best friend next to Bud—" Lester transposed, catching my skepticism. "It's funny how they both got killed when they were taking somebody on the side—"

"How do you mean?"

"Haven't I told you how Bud was cutting out on his wife when the Air Force had us stationed in Omaha? She was a 35-year-old woman, and Bud used to tell me he loved both her and his wife—but of course his wife was home—six hundred miles away."

"Yes," I countered, "—but it didn't have anything to do with his going down, did it?" I recalled that the crash that had killed Bud, the college friend who'd enlisted in the Air Force with Lester, had never been explained. The plane had just dropped like a rock—cutting a flaming gouge in a field of wheat.

"Bud—now Billy," Lester said with a slow sonority tinged with uneasiness, "—sounds like stories they used to preach in church."

"I don't think Billy even found a woman," I countered.

"Maybe not," Lester said, "but he was out looking for it." He pushed his chair back, its legs grating against the linoleum; then he stood up and straightened his tie. "I'm going, hon. Meet me at the Washington Monument at ten."

"O.K.—" I wanted to question what he'd been saying, but there wasn't time.

He opened the door and then stood there. "Bud ended up in Arlington," he said, as if in answer to my unspoken arguments. "Looks like Billy's going to be there too—I don't think Estelle's got money to take him home to Texas." He paused. "Maybe I'll go there someday myself—

He was serious, but the showman in him savored the curtain line in a way that made me smile. As he shut the door I wasn't afraid he would die—that was impossible—I was only afraid he was like Bud and Billy. For if he half-feared their fate, it wasn't because he really saw himself in the cemetery where Bud lay a little ways from Medgar Evers, the black martyr; it was because their sin was his—at least in imagination.

I cleared the table quickly and scraped the remains of the wheat cakes into the garbage. Syrup dripped into my palm, clinging stickily between the fingers. I remembered Billy drinking champagne at the Georgia Lounge—moistly exuding the sweet juices of life. There had been a fullness about him that was more than fatness....

As I washed the dishes, my mind went back to what Lester had been saying. Was death retribution? Not for Billy and seldom for other people, I decided as I scrubbed batter from the black iron frying pan. Of course, to think so might set some minds at rest. Not mine though. (I rung out the dish cloth.) It was getting time to go. (I wiped the sink even though it didn't need it.) Yes, I was scared.

There wasn't anything left to do, so I made myself get ready.

Before I left though, I snatched up the old Girl Scout-jackknife I'd carried in my suitcase for years because of its bottle and can openers. On the way downstairs I cradled it in my hand like a stone, then I stopped in the lower hall and checked the blade (it was rusty, pitted) before putting the knife in the bottom of my purse.

Outside, the street was quiet—only a few cars gliding by. Down at Esther's house, someone was repairing the third floor apartment. The three windows above Esther's were wide open, and I could smell the fresh paint. Downstairs, broken glass from the door battered by the police had been swept away, and someone had neatly substituted cardboard for the two missing panes.

I walked to the corner, bought a paper at the newsstand, then crossed the street to where the bus stopped. I found the article about Walter's murder on the page opposite the obituary section. As Lester had said, it was short—only three paragraphs. I read it twice (it told less than I already knew), then folded up the paper and got out my fare.

The bus—still several blocks up Fourteenth Street—was crawling toward me through a glut of traffic. While I waited, I thought about Walter, then Esther (who I imagined would be in jail for a long time), then Billy. Already, they seemed a little remote. It was as though they were turning into history—receding like passengers on a train carried backward from a station platform. Yet there was no time to stand and wave, for I myself was being carried implacably in the other direction—to the March.

The light changed; I was bathed in exhaust fumes and warm dust. Then, as the bus came and I got on, I began to worry that maybe when you thought the past was gone for good was just when you were most likely to run smack into it. Sometimes the track was straight (I'd decided from things I'd read at work), but almost as often, it circled back to the same place.

As the bus inched forward amidst the unaccustomed midmorning traffic, I read about the March. An article on the same page with the story Lester had written the night before said chartered trains had been arriving since midnight. From Jacksonville, a thirteen car Freedom Special. From New York a train carrying three thousand department store workers and a boxcar of lunches.

Two thousand busses arriving—not only from New York, Boston and Philadelphia—but from as far away as Florida, Kansas, Texas and Mississippi. Ten chartered flights for dignitaries. Federal employees encouraged to take the day off, six thousand policemen, firemen and auxiliaries stationed in the March area. Four thousand Defense Department troops on call. Thirty Fort Bragg helicopters ready to airlift soldiers to the capital. D.C. Jail cleared to make room for trouble makers.

At Pennsylvania Avenue and Fifteenth Street, I got off. The first thing I saw was a placard tied to a lamp post:

EMERGENCY
No Parking After 12:01

Wednesday, August 28, 1963

Fear lay in my stomach like a heavy, indigestible meal. As I hesitated on the curb, a foul puff of exhaust from the departing bus struck my face like a slap.

Coward. I almost said it aloud. I walked stiffly, following a group of blacks who had gotten off the bus with me. Peering beyond their shoulders, I saw the park ahead as an amorphous, menacing, green mass. Staying well behind because it seemed safer, I crossed Fifteenth Street, expecting at any moment to encounter angry mobs, armed police, slavering dogs....

Green leaves...the high summer smell of mown lawns. I was in the Ellipse—a languid area of graceful elms and grassy expanses that lay between the White House and the Washington Monument. Prepared for anything but silence, I was gently, almost imperceptibly, immersed in a quiet sea of people. It was like swimming in a warm wave. Placid, amiable and well-behaved, the crowd might have been sauntering to a Sunday School picnic.

The sun was pleasantly warm but not too hot. The sky was clear. When a helicopter passed over us, heading down towards the Potomac, it seemed protective rather than threatening. I'd read everything that the paper said, but as usual, reading hadn't prepared me.

A black woman brushed against me. She wore a grey and white print dress, white hat, white shoes, white gloves. She apologized. I apologized. We exchanged smiles.

At my left, a young black couple shared the placard: "In Freedom We Are BORN—In Freedom We Must LIVE." At my right, a middle aged white man—possibly a government clerk—was wearing the official March button: a black hand and a white hand amicably clasped.

Like flotsam carried on a receding tide, my fear left me. My stomach relaxed. I ridiculed myself for the Girl Scout knife—it was as out of place as in a church.

On one of the benches beneath the trees, I saw an ancient and emaciated woman resting. The bosom of her faded print dress was flat; her skin had been spotted and harrowed by age. Shadowed by a wide brimmed cotton hat that might once have been blue, her face was the color of oatmeal. It was impossible to be sure whether she was white or mulatto, and her features gave no clue. She had outlived such distinctions.

As I passed by she called me and said: "Take this, girl, it's heavy."

I paused, and she reached under her bench and drew forth a small, hand lettered placard containing the single uncapitalized word—"freedom." At Pennsylvania Avenue I would have refused it, but there, to carry what others were carrying seemed natural and right. She thrust the kindling wood handle at me, and I took it and went on—holding the poster high.

With gentle determination and polite haste, the great crowd was moving through the Ellipse and toward the stone spire of the Washington Monument. There was no crush, and within the enormous mass some had already stretched full-length under the low-hanging elms. In a green island of shade, a black mother fed a baby cradled in thick grass and from time to time fanned him with a poster that said: "We Seek the Freedom in 1963 Promised in 1863."

Like the roads in the Ellipse, Constitution Avenue—running wide and broad between us and the Monument—had been blocked off and cleared of cars. It seemed that endless green acres had been reserved for a miraculous picnic at which blacks, outnumbering whites like a soft, ever-lengthening shadow, would one by one yawn, pause and sink down in the convivial company of whites at a grassy banquet that would not be diminished by eating—a feast of every-multiplying loaves and Pentecostal outpouring.

"Move on, move on, move on with the freedom fight; move on, move on, we're fighting for equal rights," three black girls behind me sang in slow, sad hymn measures.

The girls were part of a group of teenagers wearing black armbands. Civil rights demonstrators just out of jail, I heard someone say. As I crossed Constitution Avenue and began to climb the gently rising green hill that led to the Monument, the solemn voices pursued me. "…move on…move on…'till all the world is free…."

I turned back to look and saw that the girls had been joined by boys of the same age. Maybe someone like that killed Billy—the thought struck me. I tried to imagine one of the boys' glowing, umber brown faces contorted and blackened with rage, visualize relaxed fingers clenched to fists. The fantasy didn't fit. Instead I saw the positions reversed: it was Billy who was standing over one of the boys, his hand raised to strike.

I turned and went on. Billy was not all whites, nor was his murderer all blacks. Each and all were victims of something that could be disorienting as a sudden blackout or as blinding as a thick sea fog.

Half-way up the hill, a group identified by their posters as "Local 144, Hotel and Allied Service Employees' Union, New York City," was singing: "Oh…free-dom…we shall not be moved." People were clapping their hands, and, like a drum beat, the rhythm spurred me up to the ring of flagpoles that encircled the white steeple of the Monument.

Looking around perfunctorily but sensing that Lester wasn't there, I went beyond the brow of the hill to a cluster of cherry trees and sat down to wait. Beside me, a young black girl rested near a sign that read: "What is a state without justice but a robber band enlarged?" Beyond her, a man dozed beside the placard: "Milton Wilkerson—20 stitches; Emanuel McClendon—3 stitches (age 67); James Williams— broken leg." Waking briefly, he caught my eye and said: "Albany, Georgia—that's where the Police beat these people up—"

People passed between us. When they had gone, the man's eyes were shut. I was sleepy too. I rested on an elbow, then lay back on the grass. Loudspeakers attached to the flagpoles announced that the crowd numbered 90,000. The voice blurred and multiplied, echoing itself. I shut my eyes. Immersed in the very numbers I'd feared, I felt peaceful. It was like resting at the center of an enormous heart….

"Cynthia?"

The voice was somehow wrong—but familiar. I sat up hoping to see Lester. *It was Frank.*

"What are you doing here?" I faltered. A sickening feeling of disaster engulfed me. The day was collapsing—I wanted to get up and run. If Lester were to find me with my ex-husband it would be impossible to convince him it was a chance meeting. He might take days to forgive me; the whole vacation might be ruined by anger and suspicion. Yet if I left, I would miss Lester. Somehow then, I had to get rid of Frank.

Shakily, I stood up and faced Frank. His face was harsh—recalling roughhewn rock. The furrows had gone a little deeper in the six months since we'd met in the lawyer's office to sign the separation agreement enabling our divorce. Otherwise he was unchanged—still tall and loose-jointed, his lanky body carelessly emitting energy in all directions. He was wearing unpressed brown trousers and a yellow terry cloth sports shirt I remembered washing. The right pants pocket was torn again where I had once mended it.

Frank didn't bother to explain what he was doing in Washington. "*I* used to be the liberal in the family," he told me with typical directness, hitching his familiar khaki camera bag higher on his shoulder. "What in hell are *you* doing at *this* with *that*?" With the toe of his brown, unpolished shoe, he nudged the little "freedom" placard lying forgotten on the ground behind me. His harsh New York accent, which heightened his hostility, grated on my ears as it had in the beginning.

If he had been tender, I could have turned from him. Instead his provocation held me, and at the same time, gave me strength. "I'm going with a newspaper reporter here," I told him as loudly and steadily as I could. "I've changed—" I broke off.

"How?"

I wanted to explain but didn't know how to make him understand. He was frowning—if I didn't say something he might blow up. Frank had tantrums over trifles: once he'd been arrested on a subway platform for kicking a car door that shut just as he was going to get on. When a transit policeman reprimanded him, Frank hit him in the jaw. One of his teeth was broken by the cop's retaliatory blow, and he was fined at

Night Court. The experience didn't change him. Only a week later, he had an argument with another policeman over a parking ticket on his motor scooter.

I saw his face darkening. "—the reporter—" I blurted, "—he and I are engaged." Pretending I was something more than I was made me feel safe and superior for a second. "He's made me see things differently," I ran on pretentiously, then faltered, weighed down by lies.

It was true that I admired in Lester ideas that, coming from Frank, would have seemed mere bombast. But if I was there, caught up in something so different from the small world that had once contained and satisfied me, it was because parts of Frank that I never liked—things about which I had fought with him bitterly—had nevertheless become part of me. Marriage *was* a joining, and in the breaking of the union, the parts you got back were not always your own.

Frank came from a family no more wealthy than Lester's: he too championed the underdog because he knew what it was to be one. But Frank's passion was cold—based on shared resentment, while Lester's was warm—grown from understanding colored with love. Yet if I had the "freedom" placard, it was not only because of Lester; it was because of Frank.

"You mean you've forgotten your snotty little Madison Avenue job and come around to *this*?" Frank waved an arm at the black hordes that surrounded us, "—just like that?" His sarcasm was as heavy and infuriating as ever. In pictures, (since he was carrying his cameras, I assumed he was on a photographic assignment) Frank had hairbreadth sensitivity. In words, he was a clod.

I'd been staring at the grass because I didn't know how I was going to answer. "—but I'm in love," I said suddenly, straightening to look him in the face. It was a *non sequitur* but maybe the best explanation I had. There was no time to tell him how Lester's patient tenderness had swelled my confidence, making it possible for me to accept what I'd

102

once hated and feared. My watch said ten of eleven, and I sensed Lester was approaching the Monument.

Unlike Lester, Frank was seldom jealous. My admission softened rather than angered him. "Well that's good, doll," he told me gently. "—better than us, I guess. With me—except at first in Italy—I don't know that you ever—and even then—"

Italy. My face felt hot. On our honeymoon in Italy, Frank and I had ridden from Rome to Brindisi on a motor scooter. He was doing a picture essay on peasants; it was his own idea—a labor of love. But the peasants made me uncomfortable—the men eyeing the bride appraisingly, the women pointing to my belly and smiling—wanting to know if I was pregnant yet. Soon, I hated them. Peasants were gross and dirty, I told Frank. When they asked us to stay in their farmhouses, I made him refuse. We went instead to cheap *pensiones*—the only thing we could afford—made love, argued, then drew apart—huddling in uneasy silence on narrow, uncomfortable beds....

Such conduct was beyond apology. It was late, late—too late. "My boyfriend's meeting me here any minute," I told him suddenly. "He wouldn't like it if he saw me with you." It wasn't much to say, but at least it was true.

Frank nodded, shrugged. "O.K. Why should I want to make trouble for you? Maybe I should have gone by without saying 'hello', but when I saw you lying there doll—" he stopped, readjusted the several cameras that hung from his shoulders, extracted a lens from his khaki bag. "I've got to get to work anyway. I'm doing a mood story for a Sunday supplement—two double page spreads on the March—maybe more." Taking one of his cameras, he screwed on a lens, focusing on the crowds above us.

"I got some great pictures downtown on T Street last night—" Frank broke off, ran forward a few paces, took several shots of a new group with placards coming over the brow of the hill.

Work, activity—they were Frank's answer to everything. Frank had traveled all over the country on assignments when we were married, but most of the time I hadn't gone with him—partly because of my job and partly because I was stubbornly afraid to fly. That fear had died in Mexico when I went for the divorce.. I'd taken eleven planes and gotten to like it, but by then the marriage was over.

Frank knelt, twisted, stretched flat on the grass for an instant to get the angle he wanted. I pictured Frank dashing up the silver steps of planes—traveling light—no luggage but his cameras. I saw him mounting the motor scooter he rode in New York—weaving through traffic like a will o' with wisp, turning insouciantly in front of enormous, lumbering trucks. I imagined him kicking subway doors until the cars stopped accommodatingly—opening and carrying him non-stop express to wherever he wanted. For a moment I felt sad—not because he was going and I thought I wouldn't see him again, not because I still wanted to be married to him (I didn't)—but because I coveted the free-wheeling energy that charged his life like raw current. Truthfully, I envied him.

He was coming back, but I could see he was about to go. I thought of the hundreds of times he'd left our apartment abruptly— sometimes after quarrels but just as often after making love. Still lying naked and half-asleep on warm sheets, I would first hear the door open—then his footsteps going down the stairs. He came back—but only after my desolation had hardened to resentment that rose between us like a curtain of ice….

"With today's stuff and what I shot last night for contrast it could be a great story," he told me. "There was this big white guy, doll. He must have weighed two hundred pounds. Doll, he—"

I wasn't listening. 'Doll.' That was what he'd always called me. Impersonal and belittling, it reduced me from a woman to a toy. He was as bad as the Trailways bus driver.

"—and this fat prick—a dumb bastard if there ever was one—

was buying people drinks and trying to make out with girls that didn't even—"

That was the kind of language Frank used every day—not occasional and colorful expletives but an habitual and grating coarseness. He was standing too close. I could smell the sweat on his body. Suddenly, my old feelings came back—the hatred of the last part of the marriage when I knew he was being unfaithful. Once, I'd lain in the bathtub hating , wishing he'd never come home. Then, as if in answer, the phone rang. It was Frank calling from the hospital emergency room. He'd been thrown off his motor scooter on a bumpy street, knocked unconscious but not seriously injured. He was coming home soon. Instead of feeling guilty afterwards, I was glad. The next time, I had told myself, the wish would come true....

"—he was drunk, doll—I shot the whole roll on him before he even saw me. Then he got mad and wanted to start something, but I didn't even have to shut him up. He sat right down on the sidewalk near where some girls were and then I—"

What made Frank think I had time to listen to his long, uninteresting stories about *himself*? "Don't call me doll," I burst out suddenly, "I *hate* it." I shouted loudly.

People were turning to look; I didn't care. "I hate you!" Thrusting both arms forward, I pushed hard against his chest. He was standing a little below me on the slope and, weighted down by cameras and equipment, he went back a pace or two. Then he came back, pinioning my arms with a large, rough hand.

"That's *enough*, Cynthia," he said through his teeth, shaking me a couple times before he let me go. "I let you get by with it with Mary Ellen in the movies," he went on, "but by God, I'm not married to you any more. You used to be sweet and quiet, but you've turned into a first-class bitch."

I shut out what he was saying, thinking instead of that day in the movie theatre. I had gone alone, and when the lights came up at the end, I saw Frank sitting in the last row with the gangly girl I assumed was his girlfriend. Without hesitation, I went up and slapped her. An usher came, the battle ended as abruptly as it had begun. The last thing I remembered was seeing her hurried away under the protection of Frank's arm.

As usual, I had gone to war too late, and then, struck at shadows. Mary Ellen was a cipher (not long after the divorce someone told me he'd stopped seeing her); the real adversary was Frank—or perhaps a part of me I uneasily sensed was like him.

"—and don't give me this crap about belonging here," Frank was saying. "Throw that phony poster away. This isn't some high class school picnic, it's serious. That guy I shot pictures of last night—you're like him—horning in where you don't belong—kidding yourself. He thought every black girl he saw was looking for it. He deserved to—oh _hell_, Cynthia—"

Frank spat in the grass disgustedly, turned, strode away before I could answer. I saw his head above others in the crowd, his dark, wavy hair gleaming in the sun….

Then a cold little thought began to worm its way into my mind. The fat white man on T Street—I saw what any fool who hadn't been futilely reliving the past would have seen a lot sooner—Billy—the person Frank had photographed could have been Billy. Furious at myself, I dashed up the hill in the direction Frank had gone. I went through the crowd like a swimmer against the stream, collided with a slow-moving group singing, "We shall not be moved," then wrenched my ankle painfully on a divot of grass. Did Frank know Billy was dead? Had he seen the murder?

For a moment I thought I saw Frank through a chink in the crowd—but it was someone else. Then I was sure I saw him on the far side of the hill. Just as I turned, called, started towards him, I caught sight of Lester. He was with Melvin; they were coming up the hill from Constitution Avenue. He hadn't seen me yet.

I felt sick—a hot wave rising from my stomach to my throat. If I let Frank go, it might be too late to find Billy's murderer—but if Lester were to see me running after someone and find out afterwards it was Frank—

I hesitated, and in that second, Lester saw me. He quickened his pace, raised his arm tiredly and waved. He was pale. There was something wrong. Immobilized, I glanced back at the place where I'd seen Frank. He had disappeared. Like a rising wave, the crowd flowed between us.

A light breeze was coming across the hill. Flag ropes tapped softly, mournfully against hollow aluminum poles. I stood still— waiting for Lester to reach me.

Lester came up the hill in wide-gaited western strides. He kissed me, brightened, smiled. The fatigue on his face was replaced by a sunburst of sexual vitality. For an instant he eyed me as if he wanted to take me right there. I could make love on my death bed. How many times had I heard him say that?

"I got held up at the paper, hon—I'm sorry." He paused, shot an uneasy glance at Melvin.

"We had a little trouble, Cynthia," Melvin said.

"What was it?" I had to touch Lester. I found his hand.

"—nothing much, hon—"

"Lester got another of those phone calls," Melvin explained. "This time the operator put it straight through to his desk. He wasn't there, so I picked up the phone."

"What did they say?" I demanded.

Lester looked straight at me, his face hard. "They said I was going to get what Billy got."

"Billy—but that only happened a few hours ago—how did they

know?"

"That's just it," Melvin said. "How *did* they?" He paused. "And how did they know Lester even *knew* Billy?"

We fell silent, staring at each other. Like a clock wound too tight, my mind was working overtime. I saw the evil in letting Frank go. Out of fear and selfishness, I thought, castigating myself, I had done what was weak and easy. If the same person who had killed Billy was after Lester, then Lester's safety might depend on finding Frank as soon as possible.

Turning from Lester, I looked around nervously, wondering if there was a murderer in the crowd. I would wrest the weapon away, I decided, or at least shield Lester by standing in front of him. Then I saw the idea was ridiculous. We were surrounded by thousands—it was impossible to be on guard—a shot or an attacker might come from any direction. Turning back to Lester, I clutched his arm. "We've got to be *careful*." I told him vehemently, flinging out words like sand into the wind.

One of Lester's hard looks caught my eyes and held them. "*How?*"

"I don't know—" I looked away, staring down at the grass. There was light brown dust on Lester's shoes. I wanted to draw him close, wipe his shoes as one would a child's, pour out everything that had happened with Frank—comfort and be comforted. A quick look at his face stopped me short: his mouth was set; fear darkened his eyes. To tell him then that I had seen Frank would have been cruel, impossible.

"Melvin wanted to trace the call," Lester told me, drawing himself up straight as if to shake off the onus, "but he couldn't keep the person talking long enough. Next time we'll—"

Next time…. I saw that Lester's fear was a courageous one that wouldn't let him veer from his purpose, alter his course. In contrast, mine was extreme—a panic that could foster foolhardiness, or else, capitulation. Hating my own weakness, I turned to Melvin. "What did the person sound like?" I asked.

"They wouldn't do anything but whisper," Melvin said, "but I think it was a black."

A black…. Coming from Melvin, the word fell over us like a shadow. It was not anyone there in spite of the ever-multiplying hordes, I sensed. It was impersonal, something foreign to and apart from this day—a corrupting force that, like the grave, could overcome even the fairest.

"—I've gotten calls like that myself," Melvin was saying. "Nothing's ever come of them." He paused, "It's a funny thing—the meanest calls don't come from right wingers the way you'd think. They're from blacks calling *me* a Tom. You can't please 'em all, can you?" He turned aside disgustedly.

Lester slid he arm around my neck, drawing me close. I leaned against him. For a moment we hesitated on the hilltop, staring down the slope that led to the Lincoln Memorial. It was a vast, tree-lined panorama. Green fields…green pastures…still waters…. The great crowd of marchers stretched down the long incline and across the road. Then they separated into two segments divided by the flat, bright waters of the rectangular reflecting pond. At the pond's end, the huge congregation came together again, filling broad flights of white steps that led to the pillared culmination, the marble Lincoln Memorial.

It was getting towards noon. The first part of the program had begun. A mile away on the steps, a man was singing: "Ain't nobody gonna *stop* me….Ain't nobody gonna *keep* me…from marching down freedom's road…."

Doubled and distorted by many microphones, the message was as diffuse as a vastly enlarged photograph. My thoughts fragmented. I had to find Frank—but in the crowd it was impossible. I had to tell Lester that Frank had seen Billy—but not now, not here.

The sun beat on my head. Melvin was trying to guess how many were in the crowd. I opened my eyes. Like a gentle tide, the crowd was moving toward the Memorial. Two old black men in work clothes were starting down the hill in front of us. One man was lame, hobbling with a crutch. The other was blind—wrinkles radiated from his eyes and ran down around his neck like wires.

As people began to flow past us, I was consumed by a desire to turn and run. If I could only drag Lester to a safe place—Texas, Mexico, anywhere—a place where phone calls couldn't reach us and I wouldn't ever see Frank again.

Lester drew back. His eyes scanned my face. "What *is* it honey?"

I couldn't answer. I wasn't used to keeping things from Lester. The thought of Frank hung on me like a weight.

Lester kissed my ear. "Skeered?" he demanded tenderly.

"Yes." I was relieved to tell the truth.

"Nobody's going to hurt you, hon. I won't let 'em."

I smiled. Like many things Lester said, it avoided the real problem but at the same time, caught the heart. He was in danger, yet he was offering me protection.

"You still want to march?"

"Of course I do," I told him with a tinge of anger, stung at the suggestion that I'd abandon him.

He grinned. "O.K. then, come on." He grabbed my hand. His fingers were rough. That was the hand with the scars. At age three, when whoever was supposed to be watching had forgotten him, Lester had stumbled into a pit of smoldering burrs in a cotton field. The other burns had faded, but his hand was marked for life.

The hand tightened, drawing me forward. With Melvin beside us, we went. We caught up with two old men marching together and passed them. I glanced back and saw that the man who was lame had raised a little red-lettered poster reading: "A Century-Old Debt to Pay."

Beside him, the man who was blind was striding confidently, his face held up to the light.

A surge of strength filled me. Old wounds would be healed, I told myself, and here at least, no further scars would be inflicted. We were all going together. Between a black man and a white man, I went forward with the tens of thousands....

By the time we got to the bottom of the hill and crossed Seventeenth Street, I felt better. The fear was gone from Lester's face, and we were all laughing at some little thing he'd said. It was Melvin's job to cover the speakers and big name entertainers, so he went on ahead. Lester was covering the crowd, so we cut across the long expanse of grass between the road and the pond to the side where the American Nazi party delegation had gathered under some trees. While I waited, Lester got out his notebook and interviewed a blackshirt.

Fulminating like brimstone, the Nazi shot out staccato sentences. "I object...I object...I object to the occupation of the capital of this country by Communist traitors and black rabble rousers who...."

I lost interest. The Nazi was a feverish, ant-like creature; the wrists that hung below his heavy cuffs were pale and delicate as a girl's. Like a sufferer singling out another with different symptoms but the same disease, I sensed the weakness behind his bullying bombast. If men were judged honestly and by true worth, the Nazi would fall far behind, so he set other standards. He was as ridiculous as a midget in a gorilla suit—I despised him—yet at the same time remembered I too had sometimes feared and hated because I lacked the strength to love.

While Lester finished the interview, I went over and sat under a tree. In soft areas of shade, others were sinking down to rest, and before us, along the edges of the Reflecting Pool, marchers were taking off their shoes to soak their feet in shallow water.

In spite of everything that had happened, I sleepy again. Calm… calm…. Among the enormous numbers, it was nevertheless as peaceful as if I were lying curled and secure in the high grass of an empty field. Near me, a squat, pink-faced policeman stood with his club dangling from his side. From time to time, he inserted a finger under his helmet to scratch, then shifted uncomfortably in his heavy boots. There was nothing for him to do. Sweat formed on his face and stood there, becalmed in the little ridges of his forehead. When he went forward finally, it was only to assist a dignitary through the crowd. Even then, he wasn't needed. Swiftly as Jordan waters, the crowd parted for a stocky black man with a small mustache. I'd seen the man's picture in the papers, but before I could remember his name he was gone. And with serene and imperturbably politeness—people letting other people go first and smiling—the crowd had come together again. The policeman didn't come back to his post. I saw him turn, grinning sheepishly, and amble over to one of the soft drink stands. Instead of forcing his way to the front as he might have, he got on the end of the long line and waited, wiping his face with his handkerchief, his helmet in his hand.

Someone on the podium was singing: "How many times must a man look up before he can see the sky?" Lester had finished his interview and was coming towards me. Stretching and somnolent, I stood up and smiled. Then, smack in front of me and only a few yards away, I saw a face that brought back every insulting thing Frank had said to me.

I wasn't sure I recognized him. It was a man in his middle thirties—so strangely tall and emaciated that he suggested the elongated figure of a carved
Byzantine saint. His skin was an unusual ash color instead of brown; his face seemed to be cut from stone. All that moved were his eyes.

They were frenetic, visionary—darting in all directions.

I was almost certain it was the same person. With a sick feeling of shame, and I remembered the first time I'd seen him. It was the year before—the evening of one of those grey, raw formless midwinter days that hang on in New York from November to March—one hour sliding imperceptibly into the next. Frank and I had been quarreling for days—perhaps weeks—that consumed each other like a snake gorging on its own tail. I had gone out to visit a friend in the hospital, taking an unfamiliar bus line.

At the corner where I wanted to board, a thin black driver was sitting in an empty bus with the door shut. Leaning forward on the wheel, he was impassively at work on what seemed to be a column of figures.

Politely, I tapped on the door. "Please sir, does the cross town but stop here?"

Immobile and impervious, the driver did not even look up from his yellow, legal-size pad.

He hadn't heard me, I decided. "Please sir—" I repeated my question.

The driver did not turn. Abruptly, I realized that he had heard from the beginning, but out of sheer, impersonal malice, he was not going to answer.

The weeks of inconclusive quarreling, the weather, and worst of all, the soul-sick malaise of wasted time came to sudden fruit.

"Hey!" I shouted in a loud, unfamiliar voice. "*Hey!*" I pounded on the door and kicked it.

The driver sat still, frozen in statuesque disdain.

And then, before I turned away to hail a cab I couldn't afford, I shouted so loud it echoed down the empty block: "You dirty nigger! You dirty nigger!"

Now, that very same tall, strangely emaciated driver was standing with a placard-carrying congregation not more than fifteen feet in front of me. Although children were supposedly excluded from the March, he was in the act of raising to his shoulder a boy who could barely have been three—a mulatto child whose skin was ivory color tinged with pink.

I thought of Renaissance paintings I had seen in Italy of John the Baptist carrying the Infant Christ on his shoulder and of their pagan prototypes—the Greek representations of Hermes carrying the Infant Dionysus. The driver was looking in my direction. There was no sign that he remembered me. His poster read: "Be one with God—Speak for Freedom."

My mouth tasted like sand. How could I have done that? And if I had, why was I here? Excusing the driver without question, I flailed myself.

I moved closer. The child on the driver's shoulder gave a strange cry—he seemed to be saying something in a foreign language. The driver turned. Our eyes met, caught in a single glance—then Lester came between us.

"What is it, hon?" Lester demanded. "You've got a funny look on your face."

"That man—" I began weakly, "He's a New York bus driver. I had a fight with him once."

"Did he bother you?" Lester's jealousy was instinctive and immediate.

"No, it was nothing like that—he just wouldn't answer a question. What he did wasn't right," I added, putting the incident in better perspective, "but then I shouted at him and called him a nigger and that was worse." It did no more good to blame myself solely, I saw, than it did when the paper's rewrite men turned black expressions Lester sometimes quoted into Harvard English. Facts were not changed by denying them.

"We've all done things we'd druther we hadn't," Lester began." He paused. I thought he was about to say more. The image of Esther with her hair flying around her head like snakes rose in my mind; then a group of decorously chanting marchers surged in front of us. They engulfed the driver and child, and I lost sight of them.

"Goin' to tell the President—"

"FREEDOM!"

"Goin' to tell the Congress—"

"FREEDOM!"

"Goin' to tell the press—"

"FREEDOM!"

"Goin' to tell the people—"

"FREEDOM!"

The tempo was increasing. The group was succeeded by a horde carrying posters. "What is a land without justice but a robber band enlarged?—A. Lincoln," flashed one. "No U.S. dough to help Jim Crow grow," insisted another.

Beyond posters that came like fast-moving clouds, I caught the silhouette of a man with a camera. Was it Frank? I strained to see, but by the time the posters had passed, whoever it was had gone.

Lester was talking to a teenage girl from Georgia. "I don't care how hard you try," she told him, shoving her hands into the pockets of her dress with an angry gesture, "you just can't imagine stopping at some hamburger stand and having a good-for-nothing piece of white trash tell you: "'We don't serve Niggras here.'"

"Keep on a'walking…marching to freedom land."

The music stopped and someone announced that the crowd numbered two hundred thousand. I couldn't believe it. Even if the estimate was generous, it was overwhelming. Here, coming together peacefully, was more than the population of whole towns. Rome in Medieval times, I remembered from research I had done at work, had contained only 35,000 people.

Yet as far as I could see and beyond—down to the Potomac, back to the Monument and up the very steps of the Lincoln Memorial itself—there were people—a quiet throng. If I had been asked to conceive of the Last Judgment, I couldn't have imagined a larger gathering. But it was not the last but a beginning—a gentle sea of serene faces rising with muted song. For once, the last *were* first.

Then a tall, middle-aged black woman in a blue cotton dress tapped Lester on the arm. "I saw you back there talking to the Nazis—you from the paper?"

"Yep—"

"I've been wantin' to talk to somebody like that—somebody who could tell other folks how—"

Lester was ready instantly, taking down her name, age and home town.

"Don't use my name," she told him nervously. "I've been picketing and boycotting for two years now, and I don't need no more trouble—"

"O.K." Dutifully, Lester scratched her name from his notebook. When he did that I felt proud of him. It wasn't just a gesture. Even if it weakened his story, I knew Lester would stand by his word.

The woman watched him, drew a deep breath. "I've been in all the marches," she began softly, smoothing her short, graying hair. "But just this morning something happened that—"

"—she's been jailed twice," said her son, a thin-faced boy of about twenty who had been standing silently behind her. "She was—"

"Don't you tell the man about me, boy," his mother told him. "Tell how they had *you* in Parchman Jail four months." Her hand went to her neck, clutching a thin, silver-colored chain. "Four months for going in a civil rights march," she told Lester. Her hand loosened and fell to her side, the fingers spread. She lowered her voice. "Part of the

116

time they had him in a thing they calls the sweat box—it was a hundred degrees in there—" She looked away.

Far in front of us, someone was beginning a new song. "Little baby don't you cry….All your trials will be over soon…." The voice was slow, rich, mournful. It was impossible to see the man who was singing. Rather than from the podium, the song seemed to be flowing from the Memorial itself—the three dark spaces between the four center columns marking the white marble recess where the great statue of Lincoln was. The words swept over us and rolled on toward the Monument, echoing between many microphones.

"—but what I came over here first to tell you," the woman was saying to Lester, "was how the folks here in Washington ain't like folks down south."

"How's that?" Lester demanded.

For the first time, the woman smiled. "Well sir, just this morning we were crossing a street over there and a white man—he stepped on my foot. And when he did that, he said, 'Excuse me,' and I said 'Certainly.' She paused, then looked Lester straight in the eye. "I don't hardly recall *when* a white person said something like that to me so nice."

Even Lester, usually so quick to respond, could think of no answer. We exchanged glances; he thanked the woman and shut his notebook. As we turned away, heading down the right side of the pool towards the Memorial, Lester got out his handkerchief and blew hard.

I was close to crying myself—not only because of the woman but because barriers, dikes and restraining walls inside me were going down. I was losing myself—flowing into the crowd like a stream entering a great river. When Lester found a family that had known the martyred Medgar Evers and started interviewing them, I stood off to the side trying to get myself in hand, listening to the singing as it got louder, rising to a crescendo. Then the music stopped, and a loudspeaker on a nearby tree announced: "There are an estimated quarter of a million people in the crowd...." The voice died in static. The words that came after were lost.

A quarter of a million. It didn't seem possible, yet Lester and I were part of it. I was less myself than part of him. I was not myself but one of them. Whatever happened to them, I sensed with a feeling of release and inevitability, would happen to us.

When Lester finished his interview, he started talking to a patternmaker from New Orleans. The man was seventy but looked younger—his shoulders straight under a starched white shirt highlighted by a red tie.

"Why'd you come all the way up here?" Lester asked.

The patternmaker looked at him. "Maybe this is the best thing that's ever happened to America," he told us quietly, then paused, his forehead wrinkled with the effort of forcing his feelings into words.

"Yes?" Lester was writing it down.

"Today—" he stopped and then began again, the wrinkles fading into a triumphant, boyish smile; "today is history," he said, his voice rising, "and I promised myself I was going to lay aside my patterns and be part of it."

That was the hard part—I saw as the old man shook our hands with a firm, youthful grip and went on—to lay aside one's patterns. Easy to say, difficult to do. And the old patterns to be discarded were more than reactionary laws and narrowmindedness. They encompassed a cruel, murky malevolence, an obdurate stain infecting blacks and whites alike.

Someone had put that woman's son in the sweatbox; someone had murdered Billy. The night before Lester had blown up at Melvin; the year before I had blown up at the New York bus driver. And the driver had probably treated me the way he did mainly because I was white, just as Frank had treated me the way he did mainly because I was a woman. And men *were* unfair to women—and women to men. Blacks had been unfair to blacks, whites to whites, whites to blacks, blacks to whites, and the stain—expanding beyond such easy antitheses—would never be entirely eradicated. Yet transformation was possible, I sensed as a sweet-voiced woman up on the podium started singing "We Shall Overcome," and forgiveness was the first step. Whatever I'd done wrong, whatever I needed to be forgiven for, I was part of them.

"We shall overcome someday…." The song went on—we were carried forward until we could see more of the great mournful Lincoln statue seated behind the columns, and Lester and I and a lot more people than could have been counted sang together.

"It isn't what anybody figured," Lester said with a sigh when the last chorus was finished. "Home in Texas—they'll hardly believe it. It's like a revival meeting—but there isn't any shouting—there isn't any getting saved."

"Maybe everybody *is* saved—"

He looked at me quizzically. "It's got to you, hasn't it, hon?"

I was close to crying again. "Why can't it be this way all the time?" I demanded, remembering his slap.

"Why can't you love me all the time—married or not?" he demanded harshly and then softened. "—or I you?"

I saw that the hurt of our arguments the day before, muted and overshadowed by Billy's death, the threatening phone call and all that had happened since, still lay in his heart. For a moment, I felt as if we were alone in spite of the great throng. If our love were to fail…. I had a glimpse of a personal Armageddon, and then I was part of the crowd again. At last, the speeches were beginning.

"Fellow Americans," came the solemn-voiced greeting, "we are gathered here in the largest demonstration in the history of this nation….a massive moral revolution for jobs and freedom…."

It was A. Philip Randolph—the one Melvin had said so much about. We were ready, and his words came down like cool, refreshing water. "Let the nation and the world know the meaning of our numbers. We are not a pressure group;" he intoned, "we are not an organization or a group of organizations...... We are the advance guard of a massive moral revolution for jobs and freedom...touching every city, every town, every village, where black men are segregated, oppressed and exploited."

There were cheers, there were pauses, and Randolph continued. "...and so we have taken our struggle into the streets...as Jesus Christ led the multitudes through the streets of Judea...and we shall return again and again to Washington in ever-growing numbers—until total freedom is ours!"

A great cheer arose, sweeping from the white marble sanctum with its statue of Lincoln to the warm brown river that flowed behind it. We were closer to the Lincoln figure I knew so well—the long, awkward arms terminating in heavy hands, the brooding and compassionate head hanging low over the breast—the whole image enlarged and obvious and yet, like America, capable of transcending itself.

When Randolph finished we did not push forward as people do towards a demagogue. Instead the crowd relaxed, expanded. I could see people sauntering slowly under the trees. In the green shade, some were sleeping under low-branching fruit trees and great wineglass elms.

The next speaker was young—he reminded me of Melvin. He didn't mince words or turn grand phrases. "We are tired," he flung words at us, missiles straight to the mark. "We are tired of being beaten up by policemen. We are tired of seeing our people locked up in jail over and over again.... You holler be patient—how long can we be patient? WE-WANT-OUR-FREEDOM-AND-WE-WANT-IT-*NOW*!"

Our answer—the roar of multitudes—sounded across the swift and muddy Potomac to the calm expanses, the grassy rises and the miles of crosses of Arlington Cemetery—rising and echoing in warm waves over the new grave of Medgar Evers, the five year old grave of Lester's

120

friend Bud, the graves of new wars, old wars, almost-forgotten wars, the graves of Generals, the graves of privates, and the empty earth that would contain the graves of those yet to die.

Other speakers. A white labor leader pictured the "great crusade to mobilize the moral conscience of America....in every part of America....from Boston to Birmingham, from New York to New Orleans and from Michigan to Mississippi." A white religious leader asked: "Who can call himself a man....and take part in....a system of segregation that frightens the white man into denying what he knows to be right?" A black leader reading a speech for another black leader jailed in Louisiana exhorted: "Play well your roles in your struggle for freedom...act with valor and dignity and without fear."

One speaker succeeded another, the speeches merged. Lester and I were standing at the top of the broad stone steps that rose from the pond to the street that fronted the Memorial. We could go no closer; we had come to the far reach of the tide. When a speaker demanded to "hear a yell from all those people out there," the great surging cry swept over and engulfed us, filling our throats like waves. I could not distinguish my own voice from the many.

"Well my friends," the speaker concluded in a voice powerful enough to reach the Washington Monument without microphones, "you got religion here today. Don't backslide tomorrow. Remember Luke's account of the warning that was given to us all. No man...having put his hand to the plow and looking back, is fit for the kingdom of God. Thank you."

That was me, I knew. I had started much and finished little. It was not enough to come; after the March I would have to go further, and the journey would be worth the taking. "Lester," I began, "do you think we could—"

I didn't finish the question. We were being exhorted by the Berlin rabbi of the Hitler era. "The most important thing I learned in my life," he told us, "is that bigotry and hatred are not the most urgent problems. The most urgent, the most disgraceful, the most shameful and the most tragic problem is silence. A great people, which had created a great civilization, had become a nation of silent onlookers. They remained silent in the face of hate, in the face of brutality, in the face of mass murder. America must not become a nation of silent onlookers...."

The words were steel. They demanded action—not answers. But I had been standing too long, one of my feet had gone to sleep, and a glittering, green-bodied fly circled my head and would not be driven away. And what could *I* do? I wondered, waving ineffectually at the fly. Before I could form an answer, another speaker had come to the podium. I recognized him as the man I had seen earlier—the one for whom the crowd had stood aside.

"Martin Luther King," Lester whispered, "—Southern Christian Leadership Conference."

His was not a speech of revolution and revolt but of images— calm, vast pictures receding to infinite horizons. As in *Psalms* or *Revelation*, the pictures rose, merged and were transformed into larger visions.

"...a great American in whose symbolic shadow we stand today signed the Emancipation Proclamation....the great beacon light of hope to millions of Negro slaves...seared in the flames of withering injustice."

My body told me that it was hotter than before. I was thirsty, but I tried to make my mind catch every word. The night's lack of sleep was beginning to tell: resounding sentences were carrying me into a waking dream of cool waters and green, distant places.

"...the Negro lives on a lonely island of poverty in the midst of a vast ocean of material prosperity......the Negro finds himself an exile in his own land...."

The lines at the nearest refreshment stand were shorter than before. I fought against myself, won, stayed to listen.

"...our white brothers....their freedom is inextricably bound to our freedom....we cannot walk alone...."

I knew what he meant. It was more than the black and white hands clasped on the March buttons people were wearing; it was an interdependence that meant it was impossible to oppress and at the same time be free. For like a spreading stain, the evil would overshadow the good, and all would be drawn into Purgatory. I thought of Billy, I thought of Esther, I thought of the New York bus driver. Their faces merged. Lester flung his arm over my shoulders, allowing his head to rest tiredly against mine.

"I have a dream....I have a dream...." The speaker's voice came to us like great waves of light. "...children will be judged not by color of their skin but by the content of their character...."

That was the core of the matter, I realized sleepily—the judgment by inner worth. It applied to—but I was too sleepy to think what it *did* apply to—

"This is our hope, this is the faith.... With this faith we will be able to hew out of the mountain of despair a stone of hope...."

And then, finally, a hymn more than a speech: "...free at last, free at last thank God Almighty, we're free at last...."

The songs were over, the speeches ended: we had found what we had come for. The huge crowd was dissolving—spreading towards the river, spreading toward the center of the city. The broad, stately, tree-lined streets were glutted with our gentle hordes.

Long heavy branches swayed languidly; dappled patches of dark green shade lengthened imperceptibly on the great grassy lawns. Gathered under the trees like tired children, sleepers lay curled in their private dreams. The crowd did not disturb them; we skirted the softly-breathing forms.

The Memorial behind us, Lester and I walked beside a twenty-year-old black from Mississippi.

"I'm *stayin*," he told us. "I came up here day before yesterday, and yesterday I got me a filling station job startin' Monday. Down South they pays $20 a week—here they gives you $20 a *day*." Then he smiled, stopping so that the crowd had to flow around him like a stream. "And it's free here," he added, spreading a lanky, light brown arm full-length to include the entire Mall from the river to the Capitol. "You can smell it in the air—" he signed, dropped his arm. "It's something else, man, you can put that in your paper with my name on it and everything."

We parted. Lester and I turned away in a different direction, skirting bits of white paper lightly scattered on the grass. Then, glancing back, I saw the New York bus driver walking a little behind us. He was leading the child by hand.

"Excuse me," he said as they passed in front of us," fixing me with a long, straight glance.

"Of course," I replied.

That was all. The child turned back to stare; then they turned toward a side street.

It was enough. We had spoken politely. "That was the bus driver," I told Lester.

"You and he made it up?"

"Maybe we did," I told him.

Lester and I went on. He put his notebook away. "—wonderful— wasn't it?" he said as we started up Seventeenth Street.

"Yes." I didn't analyze or amplify. I was too tired to do anything but walk. The streets were still empty of all but official cars, and there was no other way to get back to the paper. It didn't matter—there was no hurry—Lester's deadline wasn't till seven. The calm of the March lay upon us: good things would be accomplished in their proper time.

"Looks like blue skies for a while, hon," Lester continued, taking my hand.

"Yes." I believed it. The crooked would be made straight and the rough places plain. Lester and I would be married, and together, with our children and our children's children, we would....

We went on for another block, and then I noticed Melvin coming from a side street. There was someone with him—a lanky, pensive black man with one arm in a sling.

"How'd you like it?" Lester's question was half-rhetorical.

Instead of answering immediately, Melvin shook his head. His eyes were wide, as if he had seen a vision. "It was a wonder," he said finally, and then, drawing his friend forward, he added: "This is Arthur."

Arthur and Lester shook hands, and for a moment the name didn't mean anything. There was a pause, and then Arthur told Lester: "I'm sorry about your friend."

"Thanks," Lester said slowly, "I appreciate that."

Then I realized that Arthur was the hitchhiker Billy had forced from his car. Naturally Melvin had told him about Billy's death.

"Your arm—" Lester said to Arthur after a minute, "—is it—?"

"Bruised but not broken," Arthur told him. "Don't worry about it."

"You're sure?" Lester said.

"Yes," Arthur said, "positive."

There was another pause, and then, as though a benediction had been said, the four of us walked on in silence past white marble buildings with flowing fountains and green, soft lawns.

"It's almost like the millennium," Melvin said after a little. "Of course, there's bloodshed ahead, you can't deny that, but it's good to know for the record that the lion can lie down with the lamb."

Lester nodded. There was nothing more to say. We walked the last blocks to the paper through quiet streets untroubled by traffic. It seemed that a huge, sun-colored flower had opened, expanded to its fullest, and was now gently dropping its petals, entrusting its seeds to the warm winds.

Going home....

Already the busses were leaving, the trains pulling out of the station.

Good-bye...Good-bye....

Going home to all that eroded the heart of America, but nevertheless, going home....

When we reached the paper, Lester turned to go in with Melvin. "I'll be home for dinner before eight," he told me, visibly tensing for the effort of writing of his story would demand.

Abruptly, the Sunday morning feeling in me faded. I hadn't told him about Frank, I realized. "...a nation of silent onlookers...." The warning came back. I thought of the sin of keeping the truth hidden.

"Wait," I began, knowing he didn't want to. "There's something I didn't tell you—" I drew him aside, "—I saw Frank today."

In an instant, something was extinguished in Lester too. His face became hard. "What's that joker doing here? If he gives you any trouble, I'll kill him."

Instead of getting to the point, I amplified weakly. "He wasn't bothering me, honestly. We just met by accident. He's down here taking pictures for some Sunday supplement—he's going in for civil right assignments now, I guess."

"Well isn't that dandy?" Lester said sarcastically. "Why doesn't he 'go in for it' in New York?" He turned to go. "Well, I suppose I'll see you later—unless you're lighting out with him tonight instead of cooking supper for me."

"That isn't *fair*!" Anger I couldn't have imagined five minutes before surged up. Forgetting all I had told him about Frank in our long talks, Lester had in an instant denigrated me from friend, lover and equal to one of the emptiest of stereotypes—the fickle mistress—a thing with no more soul or substance than the "Rastus" of a thousand Negro jokes.

I snatched his arm. "The whole thing was *insignificant*—I don't care about Frank—the only reason I told you now is that Frank was taking pictures on T Street last night. I didn't realize till he'd gone, but he said something that made me think he'd seen Billy." I drew a deep breath. "So *there*—you probably think I'm lying, you probably think I made it up or something, but at least I've *told* you." I turned away. "You say you believe in truth, Lester, but you don't want to hear it."

As quick to admit an inadvertent injustice as he was to anger, Lester drew me back. "I didn't mean to doubt you, hon. I'm sorry. Sometimes I don't think straight." He paused, frowned, and then with a boxer's quickness to seize an opening, addressed the point. "Where's Frank now?" he demanded.

"He might be going home right after the March—but I don't think so. Once he gets started, he always takes a lot of pictures. Maybe he's going back to T Street tonight."

"Maybe." Lester didn't sound convinced. "Did you find out what hotel he's at?"

Feeling stupid, I shook my head. In similar circumstances, Lester would have gotten all the facts.

"Never mind," Lester told me tenderly, "don't you worry—I'll call around and find him somehow. You go on and fix supper, and I'll be home as soon as I can." He kissed me quickly and went in the big glass door.

He would think of something, I decided as I turned away. I was about to walk the short blocks to the Fourteenth Street bus; then I saw that Arthur was waiting for me.

"Where are you going?" he asked companionably.

I told him, and then he told me that he was on his way to the Bus Station because he'd decided not to hitchhike home. We started toward the corner together, and finally, because I could see there was no rancor in him, I got up my courage and asked him what had happened with Billy back in Maryland.

"There really wasn't that much to it," Arthur told me slowly. "I was standing at the side of the road where a truck driver had dropped me off; then your friend Billy came by. There was this girl standing a little way off—she was just a kid, but I knew from the poster she was carrying she was on her way to Washington too—so when I was getting into your friend's car, I called to her. I got in and asked your friend if he'd mind. But when she came over—" Arthur paused sadly.

"What?" I couldn't help asking.

"Your friend got all red in the face. He looked as though he was going to boil over. The girl came and got in, but before I knew it he was pushing both of us out," Arthur sighed, "because she was white and I was black. She started screaming, and he was twisting my arm. Then I guess he must have hit me, because the next thing I remember is lying on the grass with a State Trooper bending over me. Of course, your friend was gone by then, and the girl wasn't anywhere around either—I suppose she just got frightened and ran off."

"Oh." I couldn't think of anything else to say. Then I added belatedly: "I'm sorry."

Arthur shook his head, shrugged his shoulders. "It happens," he said flatly, fingering the bandage on his arm.

"I know."

Slowly, we walked the last block to the place my bus stopped. We didn't say much; the calm of the March was still with us. I thought of asking Arthur to tell me about how he'd become a pacifist and what sort of philosophy he was studying at New York University, but somehow I didn't. At the end, we shook hands. Then, after he'd crossed the street, he turned back, raised his good arm and waved.

The street was slowly filling with traffic again, but when my bus came, it wasn't crowded. I got a seat by the window. As we rode uptown, it seemed more like Sunday than the middle of the week. Passengers on the bus and people strolling on the sidewalk looked peaceful. It was as though all of us had been touched by a huge, beneficent hand capable of soothing passions, quelling fears.

As I got off the bus at the Tivoli Theatre and crossed over to the Safeway, I wished that Billy—or someone like him—could have seen how fine Lester's neighborhood looked. Flooded with mellow, late-afternoon sunlight, the block was at its best. Nondescript stucco fronts of aging row houses had an amber glow, and the brick of certain side walls had mellowed to a rosy umber. Patches where white paint had flaked from sagging wooden columns were softened by elongated shadows, and modest front lawns looked greener—as if watered by hidden streams.

From the looks of the engine house, there hadn't been a fire all day. Jim, the young, red-haired fireman Lester knew was languidly polishing the hook and ladder, and in front, blocking the driveway, three older firemen were comfortably playing cards.

People had come out on the front porches to read newspapers or cool themselves with cardboard fans, and in the alley parking lot beside the Safeway, two young men were having a quiet workout with a football. Except for an occasional backfire, the soft smack of palms on leather was the loudest noise on the block. One of the two raised his hand in greeting. I saw that it was Edmund William's younger brother, the law student, and waved back. Then, savoring the calm that seemed to have spread from the Memorial to the entire city, I stopped to watch Williams make a good catch before I turned into the store.

Inside, the air conditioning hit me like a splash of cold water. I went over by the rack where they were trying to sell the *Golden Encyclopedia* (one volume a week—$.99) and got a cart. First I bought maple syrup (Lester had used the last at breakfast); then I struggled with myself over a box of double-fudge brownie mix (there was another, not-as-good kind at the apartment) and put it back.

In Washington, I always wanted to buy more than was needed.

It wasn't that I was fooled by the pink bulbs in the fluorescent lights which made the meat look fresher than it was or that I didn't know that the shiny packages of fruit had the brown spots turned toward the cardboard. I'd read the article Lester had written about how Safeway sent the worst food to the poorest neighborhoods—and even the piece someone else had done later saying the person responsible for doing it was black—not white.

But in spite of such things, I wanted to stock the apartment, buy as if the place were ours—not just his. Lester though, saw it the other way. If he came with me to the Safeway, his face would darken when they rang up the check.

"Do we need all that?" he'd ask, reaching ruefully for his wallet.

"We have to eat, don't we?" I'd answer, and of course, there was nothing he could say to that.

Abruptly, I got tired of the store. The air conditioning was harsh, and, behind some spilled cereal, I was almost certain I'd seen a roach. Quickly, I picked up milk and the canned goods I needed, then selected the best-looking steak I could find (chuck—not porterhouse) because Lester wouldn't eat anything but beef. At the check out, the bill wasn't so much, but—like Lester—I hated to pay. One reason was that my salary was small; another reason was that Lester—even since his first-year raise at work—still let me pay for the lion's share of our food.

Then, disliking myself for thinking about something like that so close after the March, I crammed change from my bill into my wallet without even counting it. There was only one big bag of groceries to carry; the automatic door opened before me. Looking forward to dinner, I hurried back to the house.

When I reached the stoop, I set the bag down and started fumbling in my purse for the front door key. Just then I heard a shout from the direction of the Safeway. Looking back, I saw that a Police car with its red light flashing had stopped in front of the parking lot where young Williams and his friend were playing football. The squad car's doors opened simultaneously; two white policemen got out, clubs in hand. With nightmare suddenness, they collared Williams and began dragging him away.

For a moment the street seemed frozen—the people still fanning themselves on the porches, the firemen still playing cards, scarcely a car passing. Then the street assumed the specious, uneasy quality of a waxen tableau and finally, came to life.

Like sleepers awakening from their dreams, mothers and father left front porches, children got up from the lawns, and drowsing dogs reluctantly abandoned sun-warmed concrete. The first man to start to run was Edmund Williams himself. He had been sitting on the front stoop of his house reading the paper; I saw him start up, stare unbelievingly, hurry half-way across the lawn and turn back—apparently to get something from the house, for he reappeared immediately—sprinted down the steps, covering the small lawn in what seemed to be a single stride. The breeze quickly took the paper he had been reading and spread it out behind him, the sheets separating loosely—then rising to half-shroud small bushes growing beneath his front window.

From the yard next to Lester's came a woman carrying a child's baseball bat. Not far from the place Walter had lain, I saw a boy stop at the curb, strike the bottom off the Coke he'd been drinking and dart forward, the jagged bottle cradled loosely in his hand.

I left my groceries behind and followed. At the parking lot, people had gathered in a circle around the police car. As more came, the empty space around the car got smaller: the crowd was tightening like a noose. Why were the boys being arrested? (A policeman was forcing William's friend into the car as I approached.) No one stepped forward to ask, but no one moved away either.

The sky was changing from blue to purplish grey; the policemen with their clubs cast the long, distorted shadows of circus clowns on stilts.

Why did no one complain? Why did no one question? Ridiculously, I found myself grasping the door key like a weapon. The words I had heard earlier came back: "…a nation of silent onlookers…."

Were we asleep? *Say* something, I told myself—tell them they can't arrest the boys without cause. But still, I hesitated. Part of me was ready to stop forward, part of me held back—I was afraid. I dropped the house key, bent to pick it up. The door of the Police care slammed.

Before the car could pull away, Edmund Williams stepped forward. It was a delicate, almost graceful move. With one hand in the pocket of his immaculate, pearl grey trousers and his head held a little to the side, he crossed the invisible line that separated the crowd from the car.

"What's the charge, sir?" he said in a distinct, measured tone, addressing the officer at the wheel.

"Move on," the officer told him.

"I have a right to know," Edmund Williams replied with heavy politeness. "One of them is my brother. What-is-the charge?"

"Illegal to play football in an alley," the officer snapped.

The crowd sighed. It was the desolate sound of a large, red balloon being reduced to a limp shred of rubber.

For an instant, Edmund Williams' face showed furious surprise. Then as impassive mask—the mask that had enabled him to rise through a maddenly slow series of Civil Service promotions to head of his department (the only and representative black in his division, according to Lester)—again clothed his features. With a patience born of years of self-control, he tried again.

"Illegal to play football?" he repeated with measured, almost fawning politeness. "Just two kids having a quiet little game of catch?"

The officer at the wheel did not choose to hear the questions. He bent toward the windshield; I heard him release the brake. Over his shoulder, I caught a glimpse of Edmund Williams' brother in the back seat. He had been hit in the eye. The whole side of his face was swollen, and a little thread of blood trickled from his ear into the white collar of his shirt.

For a moment Edmund Williams stood still. Then with short, purposeful steps he started toward the car. I thought he was about to open the door and drag his brother out. Apparently, the policeman at the wheel thought so too. "Keep your hands off, boy," he snapped.

Boy. The word caught Williams up short. His head jerked as if he had been struck in the face.

"You black bastards stay back," the policeman warned the rest of us, and we did. Then he shifted gears, and the car slid from our grasp—backing out almost before we knew it was gone.

For an instant Edmund Williams stood alone in the empty space where the car had been. I hated to look at him, but I couldn't turn away either. Then with his head held high, his face set and his eyes hard and unseeing, Williams turned toward his house. In deference to his humiliation, we drew back. He passed between us as if we hadn't been there, stalked across two front lawns to his own walk.

As he went inside, I saw him take something from his pocket, but in the fading light, I couldn't see what it was. His front door slammed behind him, and then I saw a thin brown hand pull three, cream-colored shades to the sills of the bay window. The middle window was half-open, so the shade flapped once or twice. Then the breeze died, and there was no movement at all.

Down at the corner where Park Road crossed Thirteenth, the Police car had stopped—waiting for the light to change. As the car began to move again, I heard a loud report that seemed to be a backfire, but the car went on, disappearing in the middle of the next block where the street jogged left under some trees.

Around me, the crowd dissolved. I expected people to complain, confer angrily, but instead they drifted away with averted eyes, mumbling unfinished sentences. The woman with the baseball bat went back dragging it behind her—the wood making an empty, staccato sound each time it struck an uneven stretch of concrete. The boy with the broken Coke bottle was gone, but back in the gutter near where the Safeway piled left-over cartons, I saw his weapon sitting with its jagged end down. From a distance it could easily have been mistaken for an empty some child had brought to turn in for pennies at the store.

For the first time, I realized that I'd been the only white person in the crowd. Should I apologize, make some statement, offer help? In my place, I knew Lester would have done something. But there was no one to talk to—everyone was returning to their lawns, their porches, their empty houses.

I was one of the last to leave the parking lot. As I went back to the house, I realized I was exhausted. The heat, which during the afternoon had seemed benign and reassuring, had become humid and oppressive. Walking slowly, I scuffed my feet in the loose, hopeless way I had often seen black women do. Unfair. Unfair. Unfair. And if Edmund Williams hadn't wanted to risk his career by throwing himself forward, why hadn't I, who had so little to lose, protested and joined the boys being taken away? How was it possible, I wondered, to overcome the degrading, animal fear of being hit by a policeman's club?

Everyone else had the same fear, I sensed as I turned up our front path. They had gone back to their porches; the firemen were completing their game of cards, but nothing was as it had been. The quiet of the street had become a false calm that could easily reverse itself because it was rooted in hate. If the Police had momentarily melted resolution, they had just as surely turned hearts to ice.

On our stoop, my brown paper bag had fallen on its side. A few drops of milk were spattered on the tan concrete. Scooping up the groceries, I climbed the three flights to Lester's apartment. Once inside, I double locked the door. I was relieved to be home, but as I set the grocery bag on the kitchen cabinet I got scared all over again. There was a wet, red stain on the front of my dress!

Immediately, I laughed at myself. It was tomato juice. But how could a can of tomato juice open up in a grocery bag? I took out the things on top, found the can and saw that it had a small, neat hole in one side and a larger, more jagged hole in the other. Tomato juice had leaked through the bread, over the oranges and down into the bottom of the bag. When I came to the steak, I understood. Half-embedded in the bone was a small lump of lead. It dropped lightly into my hand, then slipped between my fingers and fell to the linoleum. As I bent to pick it up, there was a knock.

"Honey?"

I knew it was Lester, but I couldn't move. He unlocked the door himself and came in smiling. "One of the best times I've ever had at the paper," he exulted as he kissed me. "Seemed like everybody was feeling good—people shaking hands, people crowding around me and Melvin like they couldn't believe it. Melvin just dropped me home, and—"

I laid the bullet in his hand.

For an instant, Lester looked at it as if it wasn't real. Then the March day dream dissolved for him the way it had for others on the block.

"Where'd this come from?" he demanded brusquely.

"From our steak—" Quickly, I told him the story of the arrests.

"Edmund Williams—" Lester said, jiggling the little lump around on his palm, "—it's got to be—unless—" He paused. "You sure you heard that backfire after he went inside?"

"Positive—"

"So if that was the shot—the only place he could have been firing from was his front window—"

"It's only three houses down, Lester. If he'd stuck a gun out

135

from behind the shade for a second it wouldn't have been hard to hit the grocery bag."

"Sure, but why would he *want* to?"

"Maybe he was firing at the police car and missed, Lester."

"With his *brother* in it?"

"Maybe he was aiming for the tires—"

"But if he was aiming for them he would have hit them. He's a crack shot—everybody on the block knows that. Besides—he'd've had to be crazy to do something like that."

"Well," I offered, thinking of the way Edmund Williams had looked when he went into his house, "maybe for a little while he *was*."

"I don't know," Lester paused, frowned. "Edmund Williams isn't the only guy around that could have fired this. First of all, I'll bet you anything it's a twenty-two. Now I know Edmund Williams has a little twenty-two pistol he practices with sometimes, but there are people on this block with twenty-two rifles.

"Who?"

"Walter had one—"

"How do you know that?"

"Esther told me one time—" He saw the look on my face and stopped. "Jawing won't help," he said quickly. "I'm going to call Ed Williams and *ask* him."

Before I could ask anything about Esther, he was in the front room phoning. He tried once, and I heard him say the line was busy, but he kept on dialing. Meanwhile I cleaned up the mess that the tomato juice had made and changed into a plain white dress. It was a dress I didn't like particularly, but since we weren't going anywhere, it didn't matter.

The line was still busy, but Lester wouldn't give up. While he tried, I went to the kitchen and cut out the shattered steak bone. Then I seasoned the meat the way Lester liked it.

If we could just have dinner and go to bed, I told myself—half-believing it—then in the morning everything would be all right. For not-the-first time, I wished Lester and I could get married and go "home" to Texas where I had never been. Life was simpler there, I fantasized, quartering a tomato for salad. "Sin" was getting drunk on Saturday night or making love in a car parked in a cotton field. "Goodness" was getting saved at a Sunday evening revival service.

Still, I remembered, slicing the cucumber thin because I'd only bought a small one, things happened in Texas too. One of Lester's and Billy's classmates had been gunned down in his own back yard when bringing his father's car home late after a date. It was a Fort Worth crime syndicate vendetta, and in the dark the gunmen had mistaken the boy for the father. But, as Lester'd said, there was no use apologizing to someone with five bullets in his chest.

I heard Lester talking to Edmund Williams, but the conversation was short. In a moment he was with me in the kitchen.

"What did he say?" I demanded, putting water on for ice tea.

"Said he's organizing some kind of protest later at the Police Station."

"What about the shot?"

"I didn't get a chance to ask him. He was busy—he said he'd call me back."

"Oh." I was thinking about Esther again, but suddenly, I was too tired to broach the subject. I knelt to light the broiler with a match, and Lester came closer, taking a piece of tomato from, the salad. For the first time, I realized we hadn't eaten since morning.

"There's something else though," Lester said, drawing back a little, wiping his hands.

"*What*?" For some reason—maybe hunger—my knees felt weak as I stood up.

"I called Billy's wife Estelle again from work. She's coming tonight if she can get a plane—they were booked all day on account of the March. I said for her to come right here no matter what time it was, Cynthia—I didn't want her to have to fuss with some hotel. I'll take the couch, and you and she can have the bed."

I nodded, plopped the limp steak into a pan and started it. Truthfully, in spite of feeling sorry for Estelle, I wanted the night alone with Lester. But that wasn't the Texas way, I told myself as I got out bread, took the butter from the refrigerator. One offered one's home—however poor and small.

Seeing how I felt, Lester came close. His arm encircled my waist. "It's only for a night or so—" he pleaded.

"I know," I said, ashamed of myself, hugging him hard. Turning away, I busied myself—setting out paper napkins and knives and forks, turning the steak.

Meanwhile, Lester went to the front window, opened the casement wide and leaned out. After a little while, I joined him. It looked as if everyone was still inside eating dinner. Porches and front yards were empty; soft, irregular tree shadows grayed the pavement. The street lights were on, and the shades were still down in the part of Edmund Williams' bay window that I could see.

"You'd think nothing had happened," Lester said finally. "If anybody's about to protest, they're sure keeping it quiet."

We went back to the kitchen together, and I took out the steak and divided it. We sat down. He took a bite and praised it, then dropped his fork. "Billy hasn't even been gone 24 hours," he burst out, "—how can I be *hungry?*"

I kept on chewing the piece of bread I had in my mouth, but it didn't taste good. I washed it down with water, but then I felt it somewhere where it was too far down to cough up.

"We've got to eat," I begged, toying with my salad.

Neither of us did.

"There's something else," Lester said after a moment leaning forward.

I pushed my plate aside.

"This morning—" Lester went ahead without waiting for my question, "I called up a funeral home and told them to go over and take him out of the Morgue. I'm going to take care of the expenses and arrange to get him buried over in Arlington where Bud is."

"Oh Lester—how *can* you?" I knew he had less in the bank than I did—and I only had the thousand Frank had given me when we got divorced. In the fall, I remembered, Lester had worried off and on because Billy took until Christmas to repay $25 he'd borrowed when he was in Washington before. Even that had seemed a lot of money.

"The debt to my father's all paid back—" Lester countered.

"I know," I said, feeling as if I'd swallowed a stone. I thought about how poor Lester'd been in the first months I'd known him—scrimping painfully to repay his father for the year of journalism school he'd just finished.

"If I can't cover what it costs," Lester went on quickly, "I can get it from the Credit Union at work. You don't pay it back, hon, they just take it out of your paycheck." As if to show me how easy that would be, he got up and refilled his water glass at the kitchen tap and came back. "I can afford it better than Estelle can with all those kids," he told me. "It's the last thing I'll ever do for him, Cynthia."

"I know, but—" I broke off. What was there to say?

"Besides," Lester went on, "I've been thinking about it. Cynthia—if I only hadn't gone and let it out about Cecil's Bar—"

"But you never gave him the address, Lester, and besides—how could you have known he'd seen the place driving in? Anyway, if he hadn't found out something from you, he would have just kept on asking until someone told him."

"Yes, but maybe he wouldn't have found out right off." Lester sighed. "I never should have mentioned the story about Racehorse to begin with. Something *told* me I oughtn't—but like a fool—I went right ahead."

"I should have said something, but instead—"

Lester frowned. "Come on, let's eat," he told me. Then, cutting his meat as though he meant it, he added, "—we can't afford to waste it."

But we didn't eat. Instead, his arms opened and I went to him. I was on his lap and we hugged, kissed, huddled close. "Oh Cynthia," he said, stroking my hair. "What's going to happen to us? I won't hardly have enough money for myself now. We can't just go on with weekends forever."

For once, I was the one to comfort and postpone the question. "Don't worry," I told him, "we'll think of something."

I went back to my place, and somehow we finished most of what was on our plates. Afterwards though (he usually went to the front room and read while I did the dishes) it was as though we were stuck. We just sat drinking the ice tea I'd made even though the ice was gone.

"There's that new Nehru book," Lester said after a little while, "—and I've only got about fifty pages to go in *The Nigger of the Narcissus*," he went on half-heartedly. Then pausing, he gave in. "I can't read tonight, Cynthia—why don't you fix me a bath?"

I got up, taking some of the dirty dishes to the sink, and then went into the bathroom. The high, old fashioned tub stood on claw feet in the corner behind the door. I started the water, then shook in soapsuds the way I knew he liked.

Lester went and hung his suit in the closet. Then he came into the bathroom barefoot, wearing his underwear. He turned to me, and I helped him pull his shirt over his head and retrieved his shorts as he kicked them off.

"You're beautiful," I told him, telling the truth. He was perfectly proportioned—neither too tall or too short, too thin or too fat. His arms were muscular but not heavy, his legs strong, his feet broad enough to carry him a long way. He was Mercury, but his grin was Pan's. Drawn forward and down, I kissed him.

"Oh hon—" He stroked my head, then, after a while, drew me up. "Come in with me," he urged.

I'd just changed my dress, but it didn't matter. He helped me unzip it, took off my underwear, then freed my hair from the pins that held it.

The bath was full. Hot water covered with a thick layer of foam. Steam lay on the blue bathroom walls in glistening globules. He led me forward.

I had a quick view of long, tickling, light green leaves of horse chestnuts in the yard below; then we were in the water. My hair trailed like seaweed; my head was pillowed on his shoulder. He drew more hot water until it seemed we were in a boiling sea. I complained; he had his way. The water made me weak, and I was limp under his hands. I saw the sky-colored ceiling of the bathroom. I thought of plants bending under tropical, consuming rains. I was crushed against the white enamel wall of the tub, and then he was inside me—a whale-like swimmer. Foam churned over the tub sides, steam was packed hard to the ceiling. Love…love…it was— Water covered my head—I was expanding from the bottom of the sea. It was over for me, but then, just before he finished, he drew away.

Like leaves on an ebbing tide, we lay in what was left of the bath. A gentle, grey-blue-twilight breeze filtered through the open window—carrying the steam away. Lester kicked the plug; we stood up and he helped me out.

Taking a soft, tattered towel, Lester dried me tenderly—as one would a child. Then it was my turn. I started with his feet and legs, gently dried his genitals, worked with motherly care over his chest and back. He bent his head so I could daub at his ears (they didn't quite match) and rested his forehead on my shoulder while I rubbed the dark, wavy hair that covered the three little skull lumps on his crown.

Just then the tub made the empty, sucking noise that means the water is all gone. I thought of his seed lost, carried beyond me. My stomach contracted; I felt a cold, barren contrariness growing in myself. Returning to his shoulders by way of his ears, I rubbed a little too roughly. First he tolerated it, but soon, wriggling away with a little look of hurt, he freed himself. Taking another towel, he wrapped it around his hips.

Something rose between us. He headed for the front room, and I stayed behind, shrouding myself in the damp towel. Then, going where I knew I shouldn't, I went and found him.

He was at the bureau, getting out clean underwear. He took one look at me. "What's wrong?"

"Nothing," I temporized. I came closer. My teeth were chattering.

"Don't take cold." He bent over me, pulling my towel around me, giving me his. "My *goodness*," he intoned comfortingly, "just a little girl—"

His concern made me feel better. Then I felt worse. I really was cold, but instead of dressing, I went to his big chair and sat down. "Lester," I began, disliking myself, "do you remember the letter you wrote me last month?"

"Which one?" He was putting his belt through the loops of an old pair of slacks; I couldn't see his face.

"The one—" I hesitated, wadding the wet towels into a ball and clutching them to my bare stomach, "—the one where you said we could have a great love," I told him plaintively, "—like people in books—like—"

"I *meant* it," he told me quickly, without turning. He was

142

buttoning his shirt.

"Did you?" I asked foolishly hoping he would say more.

"For a smart girl, Cynthia," he told me with a flash of annoyance, "you never did have much sense."

I hesitated. I knew Lester was changeable—talking one day of going home to run for office in Texas, swearing the next he'd be editor of the paper or bust, and most of all cherishing the fantasy, the possibility, the open road. Don't push, something told me, love—wait—

But I couldn't wait. It wasn't just the fear of not getting married again or having a child—it was the fear of being left behind. For a second I even pictured myself walking alone through someplace like Arlington Cemetery. Then, instead of feeling sorry for myself, I got angry. I was fed up with uncertainties—maybe even impatient with the spider web confinement of being in love.

"Hon—" Lester was calling. His face was open, loving, more tired than annoyed.

Somehow though, he didn't move me. Instead, I almost hated his softness. Like a drain clogged with sludge, I brought everything up. I stood up, twisted the wet towels together, tossed them at the seat of the chair. "That letter was just Southern sweet talk," I demanded, standing before him naked, "—wasn't it?"

I started back to the bathroom for my clothes, but I saw his face go white. "If you think so—" he cast after me like a rock.

Chilled but determined, I dressed in the bathroom with the door shut. When I came out, Lester was getting a fresh drink of water at the kitchen tap. "Cynthia," he said quickly, the way a hammer strikes a nail, "—you don't want to get married any more than I do—" He spat the last mouthful into the sink and set his glass on the drain board.

If it was true, I couldn't see it. My mind veered to something I'd read at work about the present being the actuality between events. Was that betweenness, I wondered fuzzily, why it was so hard to be satisfied with what you had? Then I forgot that question, and what Lester had said sank in like a scalpel.

He was in the middle room getting an apple out of the ice box. The ice box was next to the sideboard, and the sideboard made me think of the story I'd read the day before. Cutting out wildly, I said: "I found your story about Speed—you're just like him—"

If Lester was bothered because I'd read that story, he didn't let me see it. "That's right, Cynthia," he shot back, taking the first bite of his apple. He turned, his eyes leveled with mine, he chewed and swallowed. "But it's only part of me—"

"I just happened across the story in the sideboard," I felt called upon to explain.

"I never got that race car driver quite the way I wanted him," he told me—as if in explanation for not showing me the story himself.

I almost said another mean thing then, but something—maybe the tired way his face looked—made me stop. He finished his apple, went back to the kitchen to put the core in the trash and paused for a moment before the sink.

I watched him wipe his hands, then something made me think of a curtain falling. My angriness drained away like a flood of shadows, I felt weak. "Lester—" I started towards him, but got tangled up with the cord of an old iron floor lamp beside the table where we ate.

He slipped beyond me like prey eluding the hunter, and for an instant all I saw was the after image of the light bulb against the blank wall.

Of course I followed, but before I could reach him, he turned and cast back at me bitterly: "You're doubting me now, Cynthia, you'll be doubting me ten years from now. Whatever way things are, Cynthia, you'll always light on *something* to doubt me for—"

The telephone was ringing.

"It's Edmund Williams," I said unhappily, trying to hold him back.

"Maybe," Lester said tersely, twisting away, "—else it's Frank. I found out what hotel he's at and left a message for him to call me."

"You *did*?" I didn't like the idea of Frank calling Lester's apartment one bit. Not that he'd say things about me—there wasn't anything Frank could have told Lester that I hadn't already said. It was the idea of running into the past in the present and maybe finding out that even if you'd tried to change—you couldn't. I wanted to find Billy's murderer, yes, but I didn't ever want to see Frank again.

"Hello—yes—*Melvin*?"

Weak with relief, I sank into Lester's big chair without even moving the wet towels I'd tossed there.

"Yes…yes…I'll come on over." Lester banged the phone back into the receiver. "They didn't let those two boys go yet, and one of Melvin's friends told him a lot of people are fixing to go to the Police Station. Melvin's going over right now—thinks maybe there's going to be a riot." Lester went to the closet and grabbed a shirt and tie. "I guess that's why Ed Williams didn't call me back," he said, "his demonstration's turning into a war."

I stood up. Immediately, there were explosions in the street.

"If that isn't shooting, I'll be a bobtailed coyote. Get away from that window—get *down*." Lester came at me at a run—his weight forced us to the floor. Stiffly, we lay in the awkward position of love.

I smelled the slightly dusty, old-wool odor of the scuffed, pink rug. I saw a crack in the ceiling that ran from the corroded three bulb light fixture to the corner beside the bed where the wallpaper was beginning to peel.

There were no more shots, but we lay waiting for them, listening to our own breathing and the tap dripping in the tub. Then, in spite of the way we'd been arguing, my body began to press up against Lester's. That made me feel better—as though what we'd said didn't mean what

I thought it did.

After what seemed a long time, Lester got up without looking me in the face. Keeping well to the side of the window, he squatted in a place where he could see the street. "I guess it's all right to go out," he said finally. "Whoever fired those shots must have gone somewhere else. As far as I can see, nobody got hit. Maybe whoever it was just fired in the air, or else—good *honk*! I didn't see them in the dark— there's a whole slew of people down by the Tivoli!" He stood up and leaned out, tightening his tie.

I peered over Lester's shoulder and saw milling forms yellowed and then obscured as marquee lights flashed on and off. I thought of a fire feeling its way up from coals. Weak in the knees, I went over to the red couch and sat down.

"Don't sit there," Lester told me irritably. "You're too near the window if they start shooting again. When I go out," he went on, giving me directions as if I were someone he didn't know, "I want you to stay in the back, and if anybody starts shooting, cut out the lights."

"But I'm not staying here," I told him, trying to make my voice sound natural and nonchalant, "I'm going with you." I went to the bureau and brushed my hair.

Lester was beside me, glaring at my reflection in the mirror.

"I can stand up to it," I told him in a voice that wasn't like my usual one.

"You can't," he told me flatly, "because you're a thirty-year-old baby."

"Maybe," I told his image, "but that's why I'm going—because I'm afraid."

Our eyes met in the mirror. "All right," he said finally, "but don't keep me waiting, I'm leaving."

My dress was damp in the back because I'd sat on the towels, and furthermore it was white. I would have liked to change into something

146

more appropriate, find my purse, put on lipstick, do all the things I usually did before leaving the apartment. Instead, I followed.

"These are my friends," Lester reassured me as we went downstairs. "They may have shot up our steak, but they won't shoot us—" he paused, "—at least not on purpose."

I hardly heard him. With each step down, I felt better. If Frank could take pictures on T Street, if Lester could defy murder threats, then the least what I could do was to go to a Police Station.

We passed the lace-curtained glass door behind which Maria and her husband lived, and for the first time, I wasn't jealous. If Lester didn't want to marry me, I would leave New York anyway and be something more than a researcher. The argument had alienated Lester, but for some reason I didn't understand, it had made me strong. Like a tide, my courage had come to me.

The door banged behind us—we were in the street. The light in front of our house was out. There was shattered glass in the gutter not far from the place Walter had lain.

Like shadows, blacks were leaving silent houses and empty porches and draining into the street. Moved by a light breeze, an unlatched screen door blew open, then shut. Lester nodded at some people he knew, but there was little talking. It was silent, serious mob— slow-moving and contemplative as if there was still something of the March in them. When Lester asked several people about the shots, they only shook their heads. One man thought a street light had been hit, but no one was sure who'd been firing.

At the Tivoli, about fifty people had gathered under the marquee. I didn't see Edmund Williams, and there was no other leader—only a singleness of purpose.

"Are we going?" a girl asked.

"To the mother fucking Police Station—" a man said softly.

"You were there, weren't you?" an older black asked me as we stood at the edge of the crowd.

"Yes," I drew myself together. "It wasn't fair at all."

Lester identified himself, and the two men shook hands. As usual in Lester's part of town, the name of the paper drew a look of respect.

"I'm going to see that this thing gets printed," Lester promised.

I knew he would, and was proud of him. But if a promise made on a street corner to a stranger was inviolate, (I disliked myself for the thought) why weren't promises he'd made to me just as sacred?

Love wasn't like journalism, I told myself, but the answer didn't satisfy. But if Lester loved a lot sometimes, a little other times and not at all once in a while, wasn't that the way *everyone* loved? Or, even supposing his love was false, why couldn't I still love—forgiving him the way I'd wanted to be forgiven at the March?

"Damn rednecks," a young, wiry black beside me muttered. He backed into me without noticing, and Lester drew me away.

For a moment I thought he might have been talking about us because we were white, but either he didn't notice in the soft, sepia light (which was jarringly interrupted when the marquee lights flashed) or it made no difference to him because his mind was fixed on the Police Station.

"Zap 'em!" I heard someone else say.

"Burn those white mothers," another echoed.

But those outbursts were scattered; most of the crowd remained silent. One man stood contemplatively at the corner looking at a folder about the Tivoli's coming attractions; another leaned against a glassed-in movie poster on the side wall of the theatre.

"Who's going to lead them?" I whispered to Lester.

"I could do it," Lester whispered back, "but it wouldn't be right. They'd say I was making news instead of writing it."

For a moment I imagined Lester at the head of the crowd. He'd do it someday, I felt, but his time hadn't come.

He gripped my arm. The mutterings were increasing, the crowd enlarging. An orchestra without a leader, we were held by a common feeling. For a moment, I fantasied I could talk to them—even lead them. Then, as though by a hidden signal, we all began to move.

Eschewing the sidewalk, we took over the street. Striding together, we brought the first car that came at us to a squealing halt. We rushed around it and left it behind, stopping two others as we came to Thirteenth Street. The light was red, but—halting traffic in both directions—we crossed.

There were more of us by that time. Calling a question and catching an answer from someone in the crowd, men came down in their shirtsleeves from front porches; women left the dinner dishes undone. Infants were snatched, still sleeping, from their cribs. I saw several men stop to smash bottles against the curb the way the boy had done earlier.

Secretly, I was glad. Now retribution. And perhaps retribution was wrong, but when I thought of Edmund Williams' brother's bloodied face, I hungered for it.

"Looks like there's going to be trouble," Lester said when we were in the middle of the second block. "Police won't stand still for it—like as not they'll start shooting. If anybody should think of getting the soldiers up here that they had in town for the March—" He didn't finish.

I wasn't worried about what might happen; I was worried about the way Lester looked. Most of the time he wouldn't look at me, and when he did, it was as though he had something sour in his mouth.

"But it's all ridiculous," I argued, talking on like a fool in hopes of lessening the tension between us. "Even the policemen must know the boys were arrested unjustly. If they don't, certainly the sergeant is smart enough to see it."

"Cops don't think that way." Lester made his way around an abandoned baby carriage, leaving me behind. "The law's on the books," he said over his shoulder. "They decided to enforce it, and now they're going to stand by it."

I caught up with him. "Maybe they were angry after the March," I theorized vaguely. "Nothing happened, so they decided to make it happen. No court would—"

"Don't count on it," Lester snapped. "This may be the Capital, but it's a southern town like all the rest."

He said something else, but I didn't hear it because we were jostled apart by a towering black man carrying a child. Was it the New York bus driver I'd encountered at the March?

The crowd had smashed two street lights, and in the half-light, I couldn't be sure. The man and the boy were gone before I got a good look at them.

We went on past Eleventh Street to Sherman Avenue where the road jogged left around a triangular, grassy area where there were three big trees.

"We're almost there," Lester told me. "See those two radio towers?—they're on the roof of the Police Station." He cut in front of me and, turning to see the metal towers, I tripped and fell.

"You all right?" He paused unwillingly and helped me to my feet.

I'd torn one knee on the concrete, but it didn't matter. Ordinarily I would have stopped to wipe it, but all I wanted to do then was go on to the Police Station. There, I felt, things would be resolved.

I started forward, but then, like Lot's wife in *The Bible*, I looked back. What I saw stopped me dead. " Lester," I burst out, "there's smoke back there. It could be a fire on our block!"

At first Lester pulled me on impatiently; then he shot a quick glance over his shoulder. "Say—you may be right—that could be my house—"

Reversing direction, we began to dodge back against the oncoming crowd. For a little while it was hard to get through, but soon we were in the clear, running hard. As we crossed Sherman Avenue, we saw the brownish-grey, early evening sky turning black as sea before a storm. As we crossed Eleventh Street, we saw the horizon tinted with the sullen and inflamed red of an unnatural sun. Then, at Thirteenth Street, we saw that it was not our house but Esther's.

"After all those false alarms," Lester said, "looks like Esther finally got around to setting the place on fire. I bet she got bailed out, bought a bottle, lay around up there and got drunk. Maybe then she lit a cigarette and—"

"But who would bail her out?"

"I don't know, hon," Lester said quickly, using his love name for me the first time since our argument, but saying it with impatience instead of warmth. "They said they were going to clear the D.C. Jail because of the March. " He hesitated. "Or else she got hold of some old boy friend—she had plenty of those."

Fast-rising masses of grey smoke were escaping from the front windows of Esther's second storey apartment. Smaller streams of smoke came from the floor above. Below, the front door gaped wide—the remains of its glass panels lying on the stoop. The firemen had already dragged their hoses inside; there were dark pools of water on the steps.

Apparently the fire had started in the rear, because the only flames we could see were at the back of the roof—small spurts rising with larger ones to form an uneven nimbus of flame. In contrast to the fire, the house looked black—its door and windows gaping emptily. Somehow, the building made me think of a tragic-comic clown face topped with a ridiculous orange wig.

As we got closer, I noticed that the smoke smelled prurient. It was the reek of ancient things being consumed—the refuse of generations, nests of immemorial mice, rotting beams, layer upon layer of yellowed wallpaper, rugs stiffened with the dust of uncounted footsteps.

Lester singled out the small, sad group of tenants and went to them. They were huddled together on the dry, narrow strip of grass beside the front walk. A man in a Kelly green and maroon striped bathrobe, a woman in a loose cotton wrapper clutching the grotesque yellow plaster figure of a cat (the sort of bank given for a prize in amusement parks), a red-headed boy of about nine, and finally, an old woman wearing a hearing aid and clutching a white chow dog that seemed to be losing its fur.

"Seen Esther?" Lester asked the middle-aged black man in the bathrobe.

The man did not answer. From a little distance his eyes looked whitish instead of brown—as though covered by a thin film. When I got closer I saw he was crying. "It's all gone," he said in a low, flat voice, '*everything.*'"

"And Esther?" Lester demanded again.

The man in the bathrobe did not seem to have heard. With a slow, imperious gesture, he tightened the sash of his bathrobe and turned his back. The smoke worsened, and a hot wind from the heart of the fire whipped the robe like a rag, outlining his stiff, narrow shoulders and scrawny, pole-like shanks. "*Everything,*" I heard him whisper again.

The woman with the cat bank came forward. "He was fixing up his apartment," she told Lester, nodding at the man in the bathrobe. "Just got new furniture and was painting the hall on his own—took a lot of pride in it." She signed, then added quickly: "Esther came home this afternooon. Heard her come upstairs singing and ain't seen her since. Maybe she went out somewhere."

The smoke billowing from Esther's apartment was no longer grey; it was greasy black. It smelled like a smoldering junk-yard.

"Burning rubber," Lester sniffed, "and Esther's got a foam rubber mattress."

Before I could ask him how he knew that, Lester was over by the stoop talking to Jim, the red haired fireman who'd been polishing the engine earlier that afternoon. "You seen Esther, Jim?" I heard him ask.

"She's in jail."

"She got out. You guys searched the building?"

"Sure, first thing, two of us. No answer at Esther's so we smashed the door, went through the whole place from back to front. Back room's pretty well gone—looked like the whole thing started in a sofa there—"

"Look behind the bed in the middle room?"

"*Behind* the bed?"

"Bed's in the corner but it's a foot or so out from the wall. A drunk person could roll down behind there and—"

"I'll sure as hell take a look—" Jim jammed his helmet down on his head, "—be some pretty horny guys hanging around if old Es got charred." He gave Lester a good natured wink and went inside, crouching down where the smoke was thinnest before he began to inch his way up the stairs.

"Hey Mr. Newspaper!" The cat bank woman was gesturing frantically at the house.

There, appearing above us like a charnel house apparition, was Esther—the snakes of her hair flying loose like furies. She was trapped at the second of three windows on the second storey. The smoke was worse in the window on the left of her—so black you couldn't see the sill. And at the window on her right—the one that had to be nearest to the door—bright little orange flame shoots had blossomed to entwine, and immediately consume, the flimsy pink curtains and tattered yellow shade. Engorged, the flames were now going on to enjoy an overstuffed chair beside the window.

Leaning far out over the sill with her arms spread wide—a figure from the Inferno—Esther twisted and writhed, screaming so loud they could have heard it at the Police Station. At first her eyes were blurred and unseeing—emptily scanning the crowd. "Sweet Jesus," I heard her mutter, "sweet little Jesus." Then she leaned so far out I was sickly certain she would fall; her magenta wrapper parted and her great black flour sack breasts slipped out; her eyes focused—and for the first time she saw Lester. "*You*—white man—" she called in a hoarse voice that lingered between a curse and a caress. "*HERE!*"

I felt him tense beside me, and for the first time since we'd left the apartment, I was afraid. Lester had more than once told me the story of how he'd rushed into a collapsing building after a Fort Worth tornado, carried an unconscious boy from the wreckage and gotten nominated for the Carnegie Medal for Bravery. Lately, I'd begun to doubt that story among others. Suddenly though, I was certain it was true. "Don't go," I begged; "Jim went to get her—and look—they're bringing the ladder from the truck—"

I don't think Lester even heard me. I could feel him gathering himself—if the firemen didn't hurry—

The firemen were working with the ladder, but they seemed to be having trouble setting it up, and Jim was nowhere in sight. The fire was worse. Pitch-thick, foul-odored smoke was oozing from the center window, engulfing Esther like a wave.

"Jump!" fools in the streets were yelling, "*jump!*"

Esther didn't seem to hear them. Her huge form had slackened; her eyes were blank again. She stared stupidly at the ground—a good twenty foot drop.

"DON'T JUMP!" Lester shouted louder than the others. In an instant, he had stripped the valuables from his pockets and thrust them into my hands. He headed for the front door.

Stuffing his things into the pocket of my dress without looking at them, I got in his way, clutched his shirt, clawed his arm. "You *can't*—" I told him over the siren of the approaching Police car. "It isn't right—she's a murdering tramp—and you—we—Lester, we haven't even had a chance to get married—"

Lester looked at me as if I were a mound of mud in his path. "That's all you ever think about—isn't it?—getting married? Well, I'll tell you something, Cynthia, we're *never* going to get married. You're crying now—you'd always figure out *something* to cry about. You'd hold me back, you'd keep me riled, you'd—" He broke off. "Go home," he told me quickly in a different voice, "go back to the apartment and stay there—I never should have let you come out in the first place."

He turned, but still I blocked his way. Our eyes caught, held. We poised at arm's length like two contestants. Then I heard Esther give a high, sighing scream. I saw Lester was going—a barren tide. I reached for him, but he wrenched away, shoving me aside so quickly I sat down on the walk.

"You slept with her!" I flung the words at his back like sea stones. "You sleep with her when I'm not here! You know what kind of mattress she has—you know where the bed is—I *hate* you—I—"

I had one last glimpse of his furious face, then he was up the stoop in a bound and inside. Like a curtain falling, smoke obscured his lithe energy.

For a moment I just sat there; then I saw that Maria the Puerto Rican was standing a little distance away with her baby. She had heard what I'd said, I realized; so she knew I wasn't Lester's wife. Her face was sympathetic; she seemed about to come to me, but I scrambled up to avoid her. Going close to the house, I stood facing the fire like an idiot staring at the sun.

We would never get married. Lester had said it, and somehow I felt that the questions, discussions, apologies and sweet words that would come later couldn't change it. *Finis*. I would be like a book with no one to read it—mere history—printed and sterile.

But if the worst had happened, there was a certain terrible relief in it. I straightened, took a deep breath. For the first time, I noticed that the center window was empty. Esther had disappeared, and Lester was nowhere to be seen. The firemen were adjusting their ladder under the window to the left of where Esther had been standing. But by the time they got up there—I took a deep breath and ran up the front steps and into the house. I remember crossing the front hall, climbing four or five steps, calling Lester and coughing. Then I had to sit down on one of the steps for a minute and lean against the smudged, grayish-white plaster wall. The plaster was riddled with little cracks—elaborate, interlocking, self-encircling patterns. The patterns made me think of the place I'd dreamed of the day before, and I began to think I was back in that place—an indefinite, grey plain that had perhaps once been a warm, shallow sea. The pounding in my ears increased, and I was standing in the center of that grey plain with a great caravan of people. Far ahead, ringing the horizon, were five hills of fire: the first red, the second blue, the third yellow, the fourth orange, and the last brown. I knew everyone in the caravan, but they were not themselves. Billy was beside me, but he was wearing a black skin diver's suit and carrying a sign which read: "Tank You." Beside him was the Trailways bus driver. There were eons between us and the ocean, but he was wearing white rubber water wings and making swimming motions as he sang: "Ban you so blue...." The New York bus driver was there wearing a white sateen bathing suit and using a Triton spear as a staff. The child that was with him was riding a whistling dolphin that turned out to be Joe the Morgue attendant in disguise. The woman who had had a white man step an her foot, the patternmaker from New Orleans, the two boys who had been arrested and a whole horde of others were carrying a flower garlanded litter on which lounged a hilarious, Bacchanalian horde of American Nazis and Tenth Precinct policemen. The litter became lighter, its bearers tossed it aside, the Nazis and policemen had become balloons, they were floating lightly upward, laughing as they rose. The fiery hills came closer. The desert was a sea after all. We were all laughing as we were sucked down into a whirlpool, and the fire flowered over our heads. The last thing I heard was a hoarse, gurgling, androgynous voice that whispered: "Wormwood…wormwood…wormwood…."

I opened my eyes, I was standing on the grass in front of Esther's house and leaning against someone. It was Maria, and she held her still-sleeping baby. I was dizzy and wet as a fish.

"Did I faint?" I asked, coughing and trying to remember where Lester was.

"You come out with that fireman—" she pointed at Jim who was now unloading a hose from a second truck. "You both get wet in there, I think. You not remember?"

I did and I didn't. It was like the time I'd almost fainted standing in a post office line on a hot summer day. I had grown dizzy, watched the room darken, and then opened my eyes to find I was still standing in my place. Naturally, the only time I'd ever had the courage to do something like rush into a burning building, I had to go and pass out. "Maria," I told her quickly, still half-confused, "Lester and I aren't married, but—"

"*Mira*!" Maria's small hand gripped my arm.

Her husband came up to draw her away; I looked where she was pointing, and then, with a dead feeling of disaster, I remembered everything. Esther was at the center window again, and this time she wasn't alone. Lester was with her. Silhouetted against flames like the time-darkened figures on a gilded Byzantine altarpiece, they were struggling demonically in a half-lethal, half-sexual embrace. Lester was trying to drag her to the door, but she was forcing him to the window. He was trying to save her, but she had gone wildly insane. She was trying to kill him.

For an instant their hands encircled each other's necks, then I saw his fists pound her breasts. Immediately, her enormous arms drew his head toward the center of her body like a vise. With Lester on top of her as if he were about to come into her, they fell back, disappearing from sight.

Two firemen were half-way up their ladder, but I was certain they would be too late. I pushed my way forward; Lester and Esther were on their feet again—close—much too close to the window. Her face was purplish, contorted, and I could hear Lester swearing, "You bitch, you black bitch."

White against black. The struggle seemed to be the culmination. Bravery, heart and perception—all the things Lester had nurtured in himself in the arid towns of Texas—were pitted against something that was personified by Esther but existed everywhere in everyone—lying like a cancer at the root of all.

I would have tried the stairs again in spite of the smoke—but I saw the first fireman going in the window. Just then, Esther rose up triumphant with Lester in her arms. Lifting him as if he were a doll, she leaned way out, and with a laugh louder than the consuming fire, let him fall. She sank back into the smoke; I dashed forward with my arms out like a woman straining to receive a child. His body arched, his arms spread wide. He fell head first like a dying Iccarus. I zigzagged, twisted, but couldn't catch him. He landed ten feet in front of me, and I was sure I'd seen his head strike a stone.

I was the first to reach him. He was lying on his back with his arms open. He was alive. I huddled over him, pressed against him, kissed him. He was half-conscious—moaning and coughing. There was a dark bruise on his shoulder where his shirt had been torn away. A horrible patch of flesh on his forearm was seared scarlet. Quickly, I fingered his head—checking the little skull lumps I knew so well. Yes, there was an unfamiliar, larger swelling at the back of the crown. A concussion? Like a frenzied mother, I felt his arms, his legs. Unbelievably, nothing seemed to be broken, perhaps because he had fallen limply—half-overcome by smoke.

As the crowd gathered around us and the firemen came to care for him, I saw for the first time in my life that there could be more to love than possession. If Lester had slept with Esther and had therefore gone to save her—it didn't matter. If Lester was going to jump up healed and betray me again—it didn't matter. I had loved. I did love. I would love.

Some loves came and went, but I knew that this one wouldn't. I was stuck with it—not only for life, but afterwards—because the thing was going to outlast me. I'd have to write it down, and after that, when I was dust, there it would be—words, words, words.

"—the ambulance is on its way," Jim was telling me. "Probably he ain't hurt bad."

"I think he has a concussion," I told him.

As if to give me the lie, Lester moved, twisted, half-sat up.

"Lie down," I begged, "honey—*please*—"

"No," he said in a blurred voice, "I'm all right." He felt himself gingerly—lightly fingering the seared flesh on his arm.

He tried to stand, but I held him back. "You've got to go to the hospital, honey. You fell on your head, I saw you. You hit a stone."

"Where?" he demanded slowly, his face contracted by the effort of speech. "I don't see any stone."

And in the dark and smoke, neither could I—-but I knew what I'd seen.

Lester didn't try to get up again. After a minute or so, he shut his eyes, and, not knowing what else to do, I stayed as close as I could—huddling over him, stroking the hair from his forehead—trying too late to protect him from what I didn't want to believe had happened.

More fire engines were arriving, and there was a noisy crowd around us. Trying to shut them out, I pressed against Lester, covering my ears and burying my face against his outstretched arm.

Waiting that way, my mind flicked to the Meridian Hill Park where Lester and I walked. Instead of the way it was then—-lush, full of leaves and heavy fragrances—I thought of the way it would be later, when the leaves had begun to turn. Then, leaf stems would grow brittle;

the green algaed water in the fountains would freeze. Eroded by winds, the statues would be shrouded with snow.

Someone nudged me; I stood up. But as I did, another disconnected picture took hold of me. This time it was of one of the lake-size sacrificial wells called cenotes I'd seen in Mexico. There girls had been sacrificed—hurled from high banks into dark water....

A long, dark green ambulance was coming down the block. It stopped in front of the fire trucks, and two white-coated attendants got out.

The first attendant, an aging white man, hurried up the walk. I got up, the crowd drew back, and Jim came over to tell him what had happened. The attendant didn't seem surprised—merely nodding as he bent over Lester. "Guess it's going to be one of those nights," he remarked finally." We just went for a fellow that broke his leg parading around in front of the Tenth Precinct station." He raised Lester's head and deftly wound a towel around it. "Be more trouble over there before the night's over—mark my words."

He beckoned to the second attendant, a young, mahogany-skinned black. That attendant brought a stretcher, and they lifted Lester onto it. He seemed half-conscious—-not answering any of the foolish, loving things I was saying to him—-opening his eyes for an instant and then closing them.

"That's all?" the first attendant asked Jim as they raised Lester's stretcher from the ground.

For the first time, I thought of Esther. The flames that had burned in her windows were gone. The fire was almost out. Light grey smoke billowed gently into the summer night, and water dripped from shattered panes. Where was Esther? I wanted to kill her.

It was too late. Two firemen appeared in the charred doorway. Their immense burden slung between them, they staggered down the stoop.

"No hurry boys," one of the firemen told the attendants as they lifted Lester into the ambulance and reached for a second stretcher, "— this one goes to the morgue. Smoke poisoning. We tried mouth to mouth, but we couldn't do anything with her. Musta had heart trouble or something, she went out like a light."

Esther's massive bulk was too much for the attendant's stretcher. It collapsed under her, and they had to leave her sprawled on the sidewalk while they went back to the ambulance for another.

I'd been standing by the open door of the ambulance—as close as I could get to Lester. But then, seeing that his eyes were shut, I approached her body. As yet undiminished by death, she resembled a monstrous black octopus—arms, legs and hair flung in all directions. Before anyone could stop me, I stood between her feet and delivered one swift kick between her enormous thighs. If anyone saw me do it in the dark, they didn't say anything, but as I turned away I thought I heard a camera click. I didn't look back. Cold and calm, I returned to Lester.

Jim had to help the attendants cart Esther from the walk. Like black quicksilver, her flesh escaped them—a loose-fingered hand tangled between their legs, a knee struck the white attendant's groin. Just as they got her to the ambulance, her head slipped down loosely— eyes half-open, hair trailing to the pavement—Medusa.

I made them put her as far from Lester as possible. "I've got to go with him," I told the second attendant as he pulled a grey blanket over Esther's face.

"You his wife?"

"No" I was beyond lying.

"Can't do it, Miss," he told me. "Nobody except relatives allowed. Come over to the D.C. General in an hour or so, and they'll probably let you see him. Don't worry—"he added kindly, "he's breathing regular."

Without knowing the black attendant, I trusted him. I stepped back. The white attendant took his place in front and started the engine; the black attendant would ride behind like Charon, boatman of the dead. Then, just as the man was pulling the back door shut, Lester's eyes flicked open.

He saw me, reached for my hand. "It was Esther," he said, nodding at the monstrous, grey-blanketed form beside him, "that—"he broke off and began again with an effort so painful my stomach turned over, "—that called the paper this morning—not some crank. Up there—" he waved a weak hand in the direction of her windows, "she went hog wild. Kept screaming about how I'd sold her down the river and—"

"But *why*?"

"The story about her stabbing Walter ran under a headline that said: "Crazed Woman Stabs Lover." The police reporter wrote the story, and I don't even *know* who wrote the head, but of course she thought *I* did it. She said she wasn't crazy and Walter wasn't much of a lover—" Lester smiled faintly, "but there was more to it than that. She told me I'd had it coming for a long time, so I s'pose she made those other calls too, and—"

The story didn't make sense. If Lester had been Esther's lover, then why did she hate him? "But I don't see—" I began.

It was too late. Gently motioning me back, the black attendant shut the rear door with a thud. "Cynthia," I heard Lester calling me faintly, "you go find Melvin—and tell him to call Jack down at the paper."

"Yes," I called back, "yes—and I'll come for you—I'll come right

away—"

Not until the ambulance had started to move did I remember that D.C. General was right next to the morgue where Billy lay. I ran forward: "I don't want him to go there," I called after the kind attendant,

"—-a better hospital—a private one that isn't—"

He couldn't hear me. The white attendant had turned on the siren. With a long wail, the ambulance moved away down the block.

The crowd had dissolved; the fire was dying into sizzles and intermittent smoke. I was left standing beside two firemen who were winding up the hose. A camera clicked—I turned. I was face to face with Frank.

"Hi, Cynthia."

"Hi."

I'd have rather seen anyone else in the world. With him, I knew I wouldn't be able to pretend I wasn't teetering at the edge of panic. After the disaster or the funeral, you go on talking, taking steps, standing erect, signing papers—building walls that are temporary, insubstantial, but which you pretend (for the benefit of others) are permanent. What's behind the walls has to be faced alone. Frank would see through all that—before him I'd be naked.

"Heard there was trouble up here," Frank was saying, "so I came to get some pictures. Your fiancé—I got here just when she was giving him the heave ho—I'm sorry—I don't blame you for giving her a kick—I hope he'll be—" Clumsy with words even when he intended to be kind, Frank stumbled and stopped.

Frank's unwanted sympathy was worse than a purgative. I couldn't answer. I stared at the sidewalk. A Niagara of tears was pressing behind my eyes, but I knew crying wouldn't be the worst of it: I was going to collapse—sink down flatter than the soles of Frank's scuffed brown shoes that I had sometimes polished and spill out what was inside me on the pavement the way Walter had—all the drowned hopes, the stillborn and miscarried forms of everything I had cherished since the divorce—not just as a child in the womb, but as bone to stiffen my flesh—oh the dying dream that I would marry Lester and have his child! I had lost Frank, but it had been like the excision of a boil—

painful but necessary. But to lose Lester through death or the decay of love—

"Doll—" Frank's eyes assessed me. *"Doll—"* he said in sympathy, reaching out to touch my arm.

I was slipping down and Frank's touch would be the final impetus—I drew back. "I'm *not* engaged to him—only staying with him," I blurted out suddenly. "I told you a lie, but what I said about being in love—that was true."

The truth was like a shot of adrenalin: it kept me going for a moment, but I was sinking fast. Then it was pride that saved me. I didn't fall down. The pity on Frank's face as he tried to tell me that being married didn't matter made me realize how awful I looked—my white dress wet through and smeared with soot, my hair dragging down my back in sodden strings. When you meet someone from the past, you want to show them how much better your life is than when *they* knew you. But Frank had come like an awkward and unwelcome spectre to surprise me at my worst—just as I was kicking Esther. "Did you take a picture of me back there?" I demanded, furious at the thought and glad to interrupt what he was saying.

"I got a couple shots, but it was pretty dark. Even if they come out though, doll, I won't use them."

I could see he meant it, but I couldn't bring myself to thank him.

"Maybe I'd better be going," he said after a minute, "—unless there's anything I can do—" He was still trying to be kind.

"No—yes—wait—" I almost let him go before I remembered. "Frank, when you were on T Street last night you saw a fat white man making a fool of himself, remember?"

"Sure I do—" Frank reached into the inside pocket of his jacket for an envelope. "I just picked these up—here he is." He opened the envelope and took out several black and white contract sheets.

It was hard to see, but as he held them under the street light,

I knew immediately that the man pictured in some of the frames was Billy. His face was heavy and a little more drunken than I remembered it; his eyes stared past the camera as if he didn't see it at all. That perspiring, vulnerable, so-close-to-being-dead face stopped me cold. I forgot myself, I even forgot about Lester.

"What's wrong, doll?" Frank demanded.

"It's Billy—" I could hardly get the words out, "—a friend of Lester's—my boyfriend. He got murdered there last night—"

"*Murdered?*" Frank looked sick. In spite of his own roughness, he hated violence—perhaps because it reminded him of his difficulties in controlling himself.

"Lester got the name of your hotel somehow, but I suppose you haven't been back there. He's been trying to call you. He thought you might have seen who—"

" I didn't—" Frank burst out before I could finish. "I told you this morning, that guy was sitting on the curb, he was trying to find a girl—any girl. I'd had my fill of him, so I went around the corner and left him there." Frank's voice rose, "How was I supposed to know that—"

"It's not your fault," I cut in quickly, soothingly, aware that shock, fear and guilt were fast propelling Frank toward one of his tantrums. "From what you say he'd have gone with any woman who asked him or anyone who promised him a woman. Look," I added quickly, seeing how upset he was—"maybe there's somebody else in one of the pictures—maybe the very person who killed Billy was right there on the block."

"Oh—I see—say, you might be right—"

We sat down on the curb and poured over every frame. In one, we saw the head and shoulders of a man, but the face was out of focus, blurred beyond recognition. In another, I saw the back and heavy buttocks of a woman. In none of Billy's pictures could we find a clearly identifiable person.

"I guess I should have helped him into a cab," Frank said in a calmer voice. "But he made me mad and I—"

"He made me mad too," I admitted.

"Yeah—"

"He was foolish—or maybe something worse," I said with a sigh, "but he wasn't bad at heart."

"Yeah." Frank took the pictures and put them away.

I saw that Billy's murder might never be solved. Dog eat dog, wolf devour wolf—it was an ancient play of shadows that was the antithesis of everything at the March.

Frank and I had fallen silent. I got up and faced Esther's building. The fire was over. The smoke had withered into white, ghostly wisps trailing against an impenetrable black sky like banners. The firemen were leaving. Their long hoses had been rolled back into the trucks like threads on enormous bobbins. The revolving red lights on the trucks seemed fainter—casting stagey pink shadows on the blackened house.

One by one, the sad little band of tenants was mounting the stoop. A fireman told them it was all right. They could go in and see what they could salvage. The man in the green and maroon bathrobe lit a match in the front hall, but it blew out. In silence and darkness, the small group started up the stairs—first the man, then the woman clutching her bank, then the old woman, then the boy, then the chow. They were like tinseled figures left over from the circus.

On the first landing, they must have borrowed a flashlight from a fireman. Its weak yellow beam wavered obliquely from second storey windows as they mounted. On the third floor, it disappeared, then reappeared as the man in the bathrobe came to the center window. Deliberately, carefully, after slowly scanning the front yard to make sure there was no one underneath, he dropped an undamaged white china lamp from the window, then a little red velvet hassock—seemingly in

166

good condition, then a gold-framed picture.

"Look Cynthia," Frank said gruffly, "that poor guy's laughing—"

And so he was—silently—his face distorted by an unnatural hilarity. "Everything," I remembered him saying, "everything." I didn't understand, but I didn't want to wait for the explanation either. I had lingered too long over the ashes. Frank was turning toward me—the same pity I had seen before softening his rough face.

I turned and ran.

For the first block I didn't know where I was going, then, after a quick glance to make sure Frank wasn't following, I knew I was heading for the Police Station. Melvin would be there; Lester had told me to find Melvin. Melvin would help. Melvin would get Lester moved to a better hospital. More than anyone, I knew I could count on Melvin.

As I ran, I coughed the last of the smoke from my lungs. I felt empty, light. Once Lester and I had raced on a beach and found he could run faster backwards than I could forwards. Then though, I could have outdistanced him. A seed of liberation lay at the root of loss. That was why the man in the bathrobe had tossed things from his window—it was the final defoliation, the last lightening of the load. If I had lost Lester—then there was nothing else to fear. I saw why the man in the bathrobe had been laughing....

Two blocks from the Police Station, I heard the voices. The first street had been empty of all but shadows, but in the last block, I was engulfed by an increasing black tide.

"Watch it, white girl," a heavy, unfamiliar Negro shouted as he sprinted past me.

I wasn't afraid. *I* had seen the arrest while he had only heard of it. Instead of slowing, I ran on and passed him, panting down the last half block.

The Police Station was a well-kept, red brick, Victorian building with a stone front. The Police Station had small blue tiles set above a carved stone medallion that said "TENTH PRECINCT POLICE STATION" in bulbous letters. The Police Station had neatly clipped grass, undernourished bushes and two light green park benches that flanked the short path to the door. The Police Station was about to be torn apart.

The crowd had gathered before the two white-globed lights that stood on black iron poles beside the front walk. Two hundred people, maybe more. I looked for Melvin, but before I could circle and find him, I was drawn in.

If anyone else noticed my whiteness, they didn't show it. We were all drawn to the Police Station—iron filings to a magnet. Fists clenched, arms waved. We jostled, we exhorted. Still, though squirming, straining against our own coils, we did not move beyond the concrete-rimmed grass squares flanking the path to the door. At either side of that door—only a few yards away but seemingly far above us—were two policemen who, with clubs raised, alternately shouted at us to "Stand back," and "Move on." Ridiculously, they reminded me of the lions which guard the steps of the New York Public Library—stone stereotypes of authority. The door behind the policemen was shut, and if either Edmund Williams's brother or the other boy was inside, not one of the stone-edged windows gave sign of it.

A foot squashed mine. A chest ramrodded my back. Blast furnace breath scorched my shoulders. Hands seared my thighs. Voices muttered in dialects I barely understood. A woman was screaming Cajun words. It was the crowd I had feared in the morning arrived at night—livid shadows under cold blue street lights. I welcomed it; I gave myself to it: "Unjust! *Unjust!*"

The policemen whose faces were too far away to see—the two standing stony and leonine on the steps—I hated them more than whatever had and could keep Lester and me apart, more than the two original policemen who had arrested the boys in the alley. We had to go. We were coiled tight on ourselves—a self-piercing spring. We were ready.

The first one to go was Edmund Williams, appearing suddenly and quietly from the side. He never faltered. He was the first to step on the grass, the first to come close to the steps. The lions above him were slow to move. He paused at the end of the walk, turned, faced us. Unbuttoning one button of his well-tailored pearl grey suit, he extracted from his breast pocket a shining and beautiful revolver.

The crowd stilled, stiffened. "The marksman—" I heard someone murmur, and I thought of the shattered steak bone, the shots in the street. Then Edmund Williams—handsome debonair Edmund Williams—with a graceful arm and a gleam of steel—took aim and shattered a streetlamp with a single bullet. The light died like a papier-mâché blue moon.

The signal. Or maybe just a gesture. The flip of the wrist in the face of years of polite subservience. Civil Service.

The cops came at him like falling rocks. They clubbed him. They grabbed his gun like a tinfoil toy. Poor Edmund. He stood straight for an instant before he fell—a red ribbon decoration leaking from his forehead.

I couldn't see him any more because I was pushing my way forward. If they wouldn't, I would. But they did, we were going. The grass was sweet and succulent beneath our feet. Instead of the middle, I was in the beginning—many behind me and few in front.

The door opened. Stone lions poured from the white rectangle of light. When I saw a policeman kick the fallen Williams, I screamed. Was it my own voice or a stranger's keening?

"*Get* him!" I heard myself calling—not even knowing who he was.

"*Get* him—" Others took the cry.

It carried us. I was thrust in front.

"Vraiment," I heard a woman behind me say, "une petite Jeanne d' Arc—"

The policemen's face was enormous—white and red—a bloated bladder—and the arm poised—

"Oh….oh…." Who was screaming?

Instead of going forward, I was being pulled back. First by the wrist—then the waist encircled. It was more painful than being born. I was thrust against clenched muscle to the staccato accompaniment of screams. I was scraped, nudged, battered, sworn at, praised all at once.

It was Melvin who held me and we were standing under an unshattered street light yards from the crowd.

"What in *hell* are you doing here?" he demanded, his voice shaking. "Damn my *ass*, if I hadn't come up from the side and seen you out in front pert as you please—a God damn *fool*. Where's Lester? What are you trying to *prove*?"

"I saw the whole thing at the Supermarket—the arrest was totally unfair. Then Edmund Williams—I wanted to show them, I wanted to—"

"Show *what* to *whom*?" Melvin was back to newspaper English again. "You want to get your brains bashed to mush in a minor disturbance that won't get more than a half a column in the paper—a crazy blonde who thinks she can get out in front of a crowd of blacks and not get pulverized into smaller-than-crap size pieces of dirt?" He stopped, spat. "Sometimes I think well-meaning whites are more trouble than—"

I looked at him. "A *minor* disturbance?"

"Of course—look—"

I turned. The crowd had broken. Many were avoiding the hails of clubs, wincing away from the fallen. A few still fought, but they were falling too.

From the side, a stocky Negro in a white shirt harangued the crowd. "Cool it—*go home*—"

At first they hardly heard him, then, moving in like a wedge, he succeeded in driving some back, dissuading others.

I turned to Melvin for explanation.

"N.A.A.C.P.," he barked. "They like to see their people *live*. Come on—let's get out of here."

"But hadn't we better wait for—"

"For *what*? You think the cops are going to carry those two boys out on a silver platter? The thing could take months in court—maybe years—" He reached for my arm, then drew back. "Say, what happened to you?"

I looked down, and for the first time noticed the long, neat, red-rimmed gash running down my left arm from elbow to wrist. There was no pain, but the blood was like cold water—it brought me back to myself. Lester. Had I forgotten Lester?

"Somebody got you with a razor blade," Melvin was saying. "You're O.K. if it wasn't rusty, but you'd better—"

"Melvin," I broke in, clutching his coat, "Lester's in the hospital—" Quickly, I detailed the story.

"It *could* have been a woman," Melvin said when I got to the part about how Esther had called the paper that morning, "but how in hell could she have known about Billy?"

"Billy?"

"Yes. She said, 'Tell him he'll get just what his friend got.'" He paused. "I know—she read it in the paper. A little piece about Billy came out in one of the other papers. Come to think of it, it might have run on the same page with what they printed about her."

"But how did she know Billy was Lester's friend?"

"I don't know. Maybe she met him before or something. Come on—there ought to be a phone booth in one of those gas stations over on Georgia Avenue. I'll call Jack and then we'll catch a cab to the hospital."

We found a gas station on the corner across from a liquor store.

While Melvin phoned, I leaned against the booth, then against the wall of the building beside it, and finally, sat down on the concrete. The strength was draining out of me; the previous night's lack of sleep was beginning to tell. I saw that courage was not what I had always imagined it—a girding, a tensing, a forcing of self into the breach—a hard-reasoned and predictable risk. It could also be a forgetting, a merging, an abandoning. The experience was no longer mysterious—foolishly or not, I had been there.

The riot was over. The crowd—those whom the police hadn't taken into the station—were rushing down Park Road in our direction. Some came bleeding, some came running. A child wailed, a woman wept. At the forefront of the uneven band was a strange, gaunt figure—yes, it was the New York bus driver, and he was again carrying the child on his rigid, bony shoulders. All in black, his eyes wide and staring, he seemed a figure from the Apocalypse, a creature of dark streets and shadows, a wraith leading wraiths. The child was holding him by the hair, frenziedly clutching dark strands as though dragging up a drowning swimmer.

Melvin burst from the phone booth, hustled me to my feet. "Come on—let's get out of here before they notice you—"

"But Melvin—I was *with* them—they *saw* me—"

"Some saw—some didn't—what they'll all see *now* is that you're white—the same color as the cops—"

The bus driver was bearing down on us like a horseman.

"Quick," Melvin said, "keep close—pretend you're my girl—don't look up—don't let them see your face. When they get to this corner we'll *join* them—run along for a little while and then fall behind. That way they won't notice so much."

He grabbed me close, thrust my head down on his shoulder. Tensed and sweating, we waited. I smelled the unfamiliar odor of his suit. It smelled like wet ink, or perhaps a dry cleaning chemical. Did

172

blacks have a different smell? I had never seriously considered it.

Suddenly I wondered what it would be like to sleep with Melvin. The thought skewered me. With Lester hurt, maybe dying— In spite of the danger, I raised my head, drew back.

"Quit it," Melvin warned, "they're coming."

I let him pull me back, and then, as the feet of the crowd thudded on the pavement like horses' hooves, I saw the thought for what it was. Curiosity. The desire to break through the wall of color—understand in a way no sentimental empathy could satisfy. And with Lester and Esther—had it been—? The crowd was with us. We went.

They swept over us—eddied beyond us. Panting at the end of a block, we were left behind with the halt and harmless.

Melvin whistled. "That was *close*—now let's *git*!"

But we did not go but waited, watching the crowd crest and ebb on the next block as they flowed south, spilling into the side streets like black foam.

"Melvin—who was that tall man—the one with the child on his shoulders?"

An odd look crossed Melvin's face. "An extremist—but one that isn't going to kill anybody—"

"I met him once—in New York—"

"You won't be seeing him again, most likely—he's leaving soon."

"For where?"

"He's a Utopian, a group of them are starting a colony in the South. Bought up some land from a sympathetic Southerner, and they're going to take their families down and farm it themselves. They may even make a go of it if the Klan doesn't give them too much trouble."

"Oh." I stood staring after the bus driver and the child. "There's something about him—" I added, thinking of the John the Baptist statue I'd seen in Italy.

"—you almost want to follow—" Melvin echoed.

For a moment we stood staring down the dark avenue. Then the voices faded and the street quieted. Melvin shook himself, and we started to worry about Lester again.

"It's an hour since they took him to the hospital," I said.

He nodded. "Come on—"

We turned right into Morton, a two block street that runs back to Eleventh Street where Park Road comes in, and were confronted by several dazed children cast up like flotsam before a little shipwrecked group of three men carrying a black man wounded in the temple. The gash was heart-shaped—blood stained his cheek like thin, fluttering, red velvet ribbons. It was Edmund Williams, and his eyes were closed as though they would never open again.

Turning to us as if in witness, one of the blacks pointed at his fallen friend. "They kicked him when he was down on the *pavement*, man—they—" Words failed him. He glared at emptiness as if still confronting assailants.

Melvin went forward to offer help but was refused. Williams' friend lived right there. The little group turned in between two sparse privet hedges, climbed three steps to a front walk that lay between a scraggly rock garden and a cracked concrete bird bath. The children disappeared.

A man in torn blue trousers and a soiled shirt turned back to Melvin for a moment as they passed between the small, white wooden porch pillars and approached the door. "Those two boys—his brother and the other one–" he spoke wonderingly, as if of an impossible occurrence, "you know, we never even *saw* them?"

The door was opened by a silent woman in a green dress. They carried Williams inside and shut the door behind them. Melvin and I were left standing in the empty driveway with little pieces of grey gravel crunching beneath our feet like teeth biting down on glass.

"We'll never find a taxi here," Melvin told me, so we went down the block to Sherman Avenue to look for one....

Later, when the case finally got through the courts, Williams' brother, along with his friend, was vindicated on the final appeal. But that was two or three years afterwards, and by then Edmund Williams wasn't working for the government any more.

As a matter of fact, the last time I walked down Lester's block, Williams' house was boarded up. His brother had left school instead of becoming a criminal lawyer, a woman I ran into outside the Safeway told me, and Edmund Williams didn't live in Washington any more. I never heard how those three men got him away from the cops the night of the riot, but if I ever see Edmund Williams anywhere maybe I'll ask him. I'm sure to recognize him, because the woman said he had a heart-shaped scar on his forehead he'd carry to his grave.

At Sherman Avenue, Melvin went out in the street in hopes of stopping a cab while I waited on the curb. As I stood there, a lanky, familiar figure hurried towards me.

Frank again. This time I didn't draw back. It was like meeting yourself one more time after a tour of the house of mirrors. And the last was the black mirror—the one that showed you naked—stripped not only of clothes and pretensions, but of flesh, even bones.

"—I heard about a white woman charging up the steps at the Police Station—" Frank told me, his rough face again furrowed by compassion. "I thought you might have—"

The gash on my arm throbbed for the first time. I looked down and saw that blood had gone down over the back of my hand, encrusting the moons of my fingernails with what looked like rust.

Frank's gaze followed mine. "It *was* you—wasn't it?" he demanded, his old, harsh manner overlaid by incredulousness.

Mutely, I nodded. There was no way of explaining. I stared at the torn edge of Frank's pants pocket. Frank's pockets were always torn. He stuffed them with everything from pointless pencils to camera lenses, adding half-wrapped chocolate bars and crumpled bills that sometimes fell out and got lost when he reached for the handkerchief he never had.

For no reason, my mind flicked back to one of the summers before we were married when Frank had come to my apartment for dinner—as he so often did in those days—climbing the long, creaky flights (I knew his heavy footsteps) and carrying a cheap bottle of wine. Sometimes he stayed over for breakfast, sometimes he left after we made love. It was hot, the windows were wide open, and the table was set between them. After dinner, as we lingered over the wine, a praying mantis, flying far from the park in the labyrinth of city streets, lit on the sill beside my chair. I'd never seen one before. An intense, acid green, it was five inches long and formed like a grasshopper. I was afraid, but Frank wouldn't let me kill it.

"It's against the law," he warned. "Sometimes they even import them to farms, doll; they kill pests."

I didn't listen. Still afraid, I took a newspaper and slammed it on the bug.

Instead of railing and denouncing me for hours as he sometimes did, Frank got up shakily and left. It was as though he'd been afraid he might cry….

"Who was the cruel one in our marriage?" I asked Frank abruptly, keeping my eye on Melvin who was a half a block away, still looking for a cab.

The compassion tinged with curiosity drained from Frank's face—to be replaced by a blank, hostile look that said: "What right have

176

you to undress us here?"

"It was me as much as you, " I told him, knowing that I had gone too far, but might, by going even further, redeem myself. "I always said it was you—but that wasn't so—"

Unlike Lester, who welcomed any opportunity to expand, dream, conjecture, Frank, even in his best moods, didn't like to probe. It was as though he carried a volcano inside him. The slightest digging could cause an eruption. "So what?" he demanded.

"I wanted to apologize." It was the truth, but it wasn't enough. It wasn't possible, on an instant, to eradicate the monster husband I had painted to myself, friends, and later on, to Lester, building the image like a papier-mâché mock-up—half-truth, half cardboard.

"I guess it was fifty-fifty—the trouble between us," Frank said. "But why go back?"

"I hope all your pictures come out. I hope you get a six page spread." I meant that too—but didn't it sound forced, patronizing? A cab was drawing to a stop. Melvin was signaling to me.

"You're me, I'm you," I blurted, knowing I sounded foolish, but determined to empty out everything at the last.

For some reason, that pleased him, he smiled. He was almost handsome when he smiled. "Well, maybe—" he admitted, "but don't go charging too many policemen——I'm not doing so much of that myself any more."

I'd felt like kissing him on the cheek for five minutes, so finally I did it. It was all right.

I ran to Melvin feeling stronger. A vague image crossed my mind of opposing figures—one black—one white—joined into a harmonious whole. I had the feeling that the memory of Frank wouldn't eat me up any more, and maybe things would be better for him too.

Melvin and I got into the cab; he gave the driver the address. He didn't bother to ask who I'd been talking to, we were already discussing

Lester—going over the story of Esther and the fire. There was just one thing left to be afraid of, I realized as the cab sped through the grey, deserted streets to the hospital. Death. Marriage was a formality, infidelity an incident, but death was the enemy with all the weapons— an archer, a swordsman, an untiring night rider who would topple barricades, invade, conquer, demolish.

As we drew into the hospital complex, I noticed the small yellow light burning on the front porch of the morgue. Of course they had to keep it on all night—waiting. I wondered whether Walter was still lying there and when they had taken Billy to the funeral home.

We got out at one of the larger buildings—the emergency entrance. Inside, Melvin asked for Lester and displayed his press card to the nurse on duty. He seemed reserved, formal—a different person from the one he had been at the March—a black in the white hospital world.

We went to Lester through long, confusing corridors. Each turn suggested that he lay buried deeper, that it would be difficult—maybe impossible—to bring him out before sunrise. If he was badly hurt, I wanted to take him to a better hospital. If he wasn't, I wanted to take him home.

Lester's room was small, anti-climactic—a windowless, two-bedded cell where he lay alone on the white slab of a sheet, his head entombed in bandages. His eyes were shut.

"Lester—" I went in first—scared, but at the same time crazy to strip away the sheets and windings, kiss him into consciousness, get him to walk, run, escape from the hospital, even Melvin—go home.

Just as I got to him, Lester came to life—grinned, sat up and reached for the newspaper on the bed stand as if to show us he'd only been resting for a moment.

"Hi Cynthia. Hi Mel." Lester's voice was a strained imitation of his usual exuberance. In spite of the falseness, he drew me in, his eyes appraising my thoughts. He saw that I was afraid and began setting up barriers against it—partly to keep me at a distance and partly because he was afraid too.

"That bitch almost got the best of me," he told Melvin in the same, man-to-man manner he'd used with Billy the night before. "I always said some hare-brained, split tailed broad would be the death of me," he smiled; "—but I hoped it would be in bed."

He was shutting me out by turning everything to jokes and stereotypes, but I wasn't going to let him. "Honey," I began, putting my hand on his shoulder, trying to make him lie back, "did they x-ray your head?"

"They wanted to, but I wouldn't let 'em." He smiled again. He smiled again. "It's just a bump, and I didn't want them messing with it. X-rays can hurt your genes. I got hold of Edmund Williams' wife—she works down here, you know. She got me a release to sign, and I signed it. Then they fixed up my arm just fine." He fingered the bandage, giving me a look that was half-rebellious, half-contrite. "It still kind of feels like it's on fire, he admitted. "Say, "he went on, putting things together more slowly than he usually did, "what happened—did Ed Williams go over to the Police Station?"

I told Lester about the riot—leaving out the part about what I'd done and ending up with the three men carrying Edmund Williams into the house.

Lester whistled, then shook his head. "Ed must have gone clear out of his mind. His wife told me that when she had to leave for work he was just sitting in the front room with the lights out, holding a twenty-two. She tried to take it away from him, but he wouldn't let her."

"The shades were down before we heard that shot in the street," I said. "Did he fire that? He shot out the street light at the Police Station—did he break the one in front of our house too? Was he the one who hit our steak?"

"If he did some of those things, nobody saw him," Lester said. "Besides," he went on, talking more quickly than usual, "why would a crack marksman want to shoot his own street light—or our grocery bag? If he'd wanted to kill one of those policemen at the station house, he could have done it easy as pie."

I thought of the sound when the street light at the Police Station shattered—ice breaking on a winter pond. I remembered the man in the green and maroon bathrobe dropping the unbroken white china lamp from the third storey window. "Maybe Edmund Williams just felt like breaking things," I said.

"You'd better lie back, man," Melvin cut in, coming to the foot of Lester's bed. "You don't look so good."

Melvin was right. Lester's eyes were glazed, his face feverish. He lay back on one elbow hesitating, looking from me to Melvin and back to me again.

"Why don't you stay *here* tonight, Les," Melvin said. "Then tomorrow, we'll take you home or to a better hospital the way Cynthia wants. We'll all get some rest first;" he nodded at me, "—she's been through something too."

Before I could stop him he told Lester about my charging up the steps at the Police Station. It wasn't that I didn't want Lester to know, it was just that I didn't think it was the right time to tell him. It wasn't.

Lester sat bolt upright instead of lying back. "*You* did that?" he demanded, looking proud of me but at the same time regretful that he hadn't been there to do more and better himself. He started to smile at me, but then his eyes got blank. He leaned dangerously to one side of the bed, but Melvin eased him down.

"Take it easy, man," Melvin warned.

"*Please*, Lester," I begged, my voice rising in the same querulous way it did when we argued. "You can't go anywhere unless an x-ray shows your head's all right."

I shouldn't have said that.

He raised his head and looked at me with distaste. "Hell, honey, I can't stay *here* any more." He sat up again with an effort so painful I wanted to look away. "I was just waiting for you to come and get me." He was half-boasting, half-telling the truth, trying out an idea which had been fantasy before we entered the room.

"But Lester—-what if you've got a concussion? What if—"

The more I argued, the stronger he got. I saw I was making another mistake—a mistake that might even be a worse one than nagging him to get married—I had put his manhood in question in front of Melvin. To prove that he was not one to weakly cater to a woman's whims, he was going to leave the hospital no matter what.

"—Melvin was in a car wreck a couple of months ago, and he came right in to work with a banged-up nose and met his deadline," Lester was saying. His eyes were bloodshot—his hands trembled, but he jerked back the bed sheet and thrust his newspaper at me. "Here— take a look at the first edition while I dress."

The color of his face when his feet hit the floor made me sick. But his eyes held me off; he wouldn't let me help him. Behind the hardness, there were other Lester's. One was sexual—still capable, if there were only a moment of privacy, of pulling me to the bed and pushing me down beneath him. Another was gentle and tender—ready to fold away my soot-smeared dress, bathe the slash on my arm that he'd seen but not acknowledged. Still another was vulnerable—wanting to be mothered—longing to curl close and sleep.

He took his things out of the locker next to the bed and went into the little lavatory just inside the door.

Melvin sat on the chair, I perched on the bed. "I knew a guy down home that got his skull fractured falling off a mule," Melvin said. "He came to for an hour or two, and everybody thought he was all right—but it turned out he'd torn an artery in his brain. That very same day, a little while later, he just fell down dead."

"Tell him," I begged, whispering because I knew Lester would be angry if he heard us.

We waited in uncomfortable silence for Lester to come out. The paper lay on the bed beside me, and I saw Lester's story printed next to Melvin's on the front page. I couldn't read it. The March seemed long past. Dreams weren't enough.

When Lester came out of the bathroom, I was almost sure he'd vomited. His face was whiter than the wall, his eyes glassy. When he leaned over to pick up the newspaper from the floor where I'd dropped it, he staggered against Melvin and almost fell.

"Look—" Melvin began, "are you sure you ought to go home tonight?"

"Come on—" was all Lester answered.

Before Melvin could tell him about the man back home, Lester was leading us through the white corridors. It was the opposite of what I'd imagined—not my releasing him. Instead, he was dragging us—a pale Orpheus.

Still—even though I had the feeling it was wrong—I didn't try to stop him. Instead, I was dreaming of when we'd be home and could (if Billy's wife Estelle didn't arrive) lie down to sleep in each other's arms. Then, I fantasized, the anger between us would scatter like ashes and—

We stopped at the nurse's desk, and somehow, Lester signed himself out of the hospital. Then a steel-rimmed revolving door carried us outside. Leaving the dark brick building behind us, we crossed a shadowy, grass-covered plot. The morgue was off at our left—it's light still burning. There was just one dilapidated-looking taxi waiting, and Melvin had to wake the driver. Brushing aside our efforts to help him, Lester got in and we followed.

For a block or so, Lester smiled and joked with Melvin. After that though, he lay back with his eyes shut, his head swaying loosely against the black vinyl seat. If Melvin hadn't been there, I would have made Lester put his head in my lap. Since he was, I held Lester's hand—staring out at the empty streets and worrying.

We passed the Capitol, we sped along the Mall—windows open to the whitening night. I smelled moist earth, green leaves, grass bent by a quarter of a million marcher's feet. They had gone, and with the morning sun the grass would rise, straighten—almost as if they had never marched.

We dropped Melvin at the paper, then turned up Fourteenth Street, going home. To Melvin, Lester swore he'd be down at the paper in the morning "sure as hell." When we were alone though, Lester reached out, drew me close and admitted: "I'm tired, hon—so tired." He looked at me, reading my face. "Don't be mad at me for leaving the hospital, Cynthia. It was lonely—I wanted to be home with you."

"Yes, yes...." I couldn't say more.

"Oh baby—" his tenderness melted me. He was once more the Lester I loved most—burying his face in my shoulder.

I promised myself he was going to be all right. I planned how I would feed him nourishing food, make him stay in bed for a week, and if necessary, take all the money I had—the thousand dollars Frank had given me when we were divorced—to pay the best brain specialist in Washington to see Lester. I planned until I got tired, then I let my head fall back. We rested against each other—drawing strength.

As the old, rattling cab carried us through long, grey streets, I remembered the first ride we'd taken to the beach where we'd made love. The beginning of our journey. For the second time that night, I thought of a curtain falling. The thought made me open my eyes. We both sat up. We were only a few blocks from home.

"I'm sorry Esther's dead," Lester said softly, as if speaking of a friend.

"How could you be? She tried to kill you."

"Almost did it too—but she was a good girl when she was sober. Lately though, she was hardly ever sober." He paused, eyed me guardedly—evaluating my mood. "Last summer," he began finally, keeping his voice low so the driver couldn't hear, "the first time Billy came to Washington, it was like last night, hon—he wanted a black girl."

I nodded.

"I'd heard what Esther was like from guys on the block, and I'd been up to see her a couple of times getting leads for stories. She knew what was going on—men told her things. That night I called her, and she said come on. Walter was down south somewhere, and she hadn't seen him for weeks. Billy brought some beer he had, and for a while the three of us just sat there drinking and talking. Then old Bill got hot, borrowed $25 from me because he'd left his wallet back at the apartment, and took her into the bedroom. I just sat there with my beer—waiting for what was supposed to be my turn and feeling bad. You see, it was the week right after I met you—no—don't look that way-" he took my hand and held it hard. It was as if we were being drawn up to the top of a roller coaster—waiting for the first sickening drop.

"When Bill came out carrying his shirt," Lester went on, "I didn't see how I was going to go through with it, but I didn't see how I was going to get out of it either. So I went in, and there she was—sprawled out buck naked like an old black octopus. She pulled me down on the bed beside her—-it was like sinking into a cotton ball. I hate foam rubber—-that's how I remembered about her mattress at the fire. The whole bed smelled sweet and stale—like talcum powder somebody spilled last week. She was pretty drunk by then, and she tried to drag me onto her. Maybe you won't understand this, but with her lying there like that I guess I'd just've gone ahead and done it if it hadn't been for you."

"For me?"

"Instead of doing what she wanted I told her about you, and before I got through I found out I wasn't just saying it so I could get you off my conscience and go ahead—I loved you. I'd picked up girls lots of times before and forgot them just as fast, but you—you were like a stone I'd found on the beach that turned out to be something valuable."

"But you *said* you loved me before that. You said you loved me three days after the night on the beach."

He smiled. "Saying isn't the same thing as being sure. Haven't you learned that yet?"

The words cut. I couldn't answer. I saw how exhausted he looked. I thought of how I'd taken words he'd used to launch, then speed, his love—winds puffing white sails—and tried to turn them into mechanical breezes that would carry us straight to marriage, the snug harbor, with never a jibe or a tack.

If we weren't going to have the "great love" he'd written me a letter about, I saw, it was my fault as much as his. Besides, there wasn't a way in the world to make love secure against time and chance. To try was setting out to autopsy life itself. Like marchers, lovers had to live on dreams. And when dreams failed—the marchers coming home to the arrests at the supermarket and then fruitlessly demanding justice at the Police Station—the only hope was to take up hope.

With the suddenness of a fever, I got sleepy. More than anything, I wanted to let my eyes shut, sleep, and dream again.

"Esther always acted afterwards like I *had*," Lester told me as we turned into the last block. "—used to ask me when I was coming up for some more if she met me on the street—or else say something dirty. I never paid much mind to it, but I knew she was *mad*. She couldn't get the better of me, and that made her want to. Walter came home in the winter, and then it eased off for a while. Since spring though, he's been gone off and on, and she's had guys up there all the time. Maybe she'd've liked Walter to use that old twenty-two he had to keep the others off. But of course he *didn't*—he just left it there. I suppose that's what got to her—he didn't give a damn and she knew it. Lately too, I was beginning to think Walter had maybe gotten her into pills or something. I never had time to check it out, but I kind of thought he might be starting up that kind of business. If so—Es most likely hated him for it. Maybe that was why she let him have it in the end. Whatever it was, she'd been drinking for years, and lately she was just plain crazy—turning in false alarms and all that. I tried to tell her to stop it yesterday—but of course she wouldn't listen. Just seeing me sent her off like a rocket."

The cab stopped close to the curb. We were home. Lester got out slowly, and I helped him up the three little steps that led to the front path. Then, glancing left, I noticed Esther's house. It looked horrible. There were no lights in the half-charred skeleton: I wondered whether the tenants had gone somewhere for the night. Despite her death, it seemed that Esther still lived there.

We went up our front walk more slowly than we ever had in our lives. Lester—who usually covered the distance in seconds, taking the steps two at a time—was leaning on me heavily. His right leg buckled once; he almost fell. His right arm lay across my back like a weight, the hand dangling limply from my shoulder. I wondered if we would ever reach the front door—let alone navigate the long flight to the apartment. Although the sky was almost white, black birds on the telephone wires chattering for dawn, I felt as if the day were ending instead of beginning. A far-reaching midnight tide seemed to be flowing to us from Esther's house. It dragged at our feet, swirled at our ankles, rose to our knees.

"Do you mind a lot—" Lester asked, panting as if he'd been climbing a hill, "–about me going over to Esther's with Billy and all?"

"No," I told him, "—I don't." the day before that would have been a lie; then it wasn't.

He stopped to rest; I kissed his cheek. I was beginning to

think that courage was something more than charging a Police Station. Maybe courage also was accepting things as they were. And evil, I was almost sure, was a lot less simple than wanting to sleep with someone. Wasn't it sometimes the lust for certainty, the promiscuous acceptance of stereotypes?

"—-the funny thing is," Lester said, taking a few more steps, "that even though I *didn't* do it with Es, I felt responsible—-as if Billy's sin was mine. Maybe you *are* your brother's keeper—-like the preachers say."

We stopped to rest again. His weight was a mountain against me.

"Es knew she had a hold on me," he went on slowly. "That's why she called me from the window like she did-—the way you'd call a dog."

We went on. A step and then a rest. A step and then a longer rest.

I loved him, and we were almost home. I would always love him.

When we finally got to the stoop, he was too heavy for me to hold.

He stumbled at the first step. Pitched forward so fast I couldn't catch him. Sprawled over six insignificant grey steps.

When I got down beside him and cradled his head against me, I saw the blood coming from his mouth. First the trickle, then the flood.

He was muttering . "Go…to sleepy…." Half-conscious, I think he saw the situation reversed, believed he was comforting me with the pony lullaby in bed, before sleep, as he often had.

His voice faded. The blood came down on my sooty white dress. His eyes focused on the burnt-out house, the fading moon, then me.

"Lester," I begged, shouting so he'd hear me, "take me with you—"

He couldn't. There's no talking to the tide. His grasp relaxed, his neck went limp. Before I felt his heart, I knew he was gone.

There was a white woman coming up the walk with a suitcase. Billy's wife. It had to be.

I turned away, buried my head in Lester's chest, clutching his hair in my hands. Already I was fighting time—the minutes—inevitably turning into hours, days, years—that would separate me from the living Lester. Maybe I'd go to Texas—traveling to places he'd talked about.

Ride a bright and shining pony.

Whatever that meant, I'd probably be running into other things that weren't white or black, but instead, surpassed stereotypes. And maybe to head west, I decided as the tears finally came, was just what Lester would have wanted.

BOOKS BY ELISABETH STEVENS

I. POETRY:

Sirens' Songs, Baltimore, BrickHouse Books, 2011.

Sirens' Songs (*Livre d'Artiste*), Sarasota, Goss Press, 2010.

Ragbag, Sarasota, Peppertree Press, 2010.

Household Words, Sarasota, Goss Press, Second Edition,2009.

Household Words, Baltimore, Three Conditions Press, First Edition, 2000.

The Night Lover, Delhi, Birch Brook Press, 1995.

Children of Dust: Portraits & Preludes, Baltimore, New Poets Series,. 1983

II. FICTION:

Ride a Bright and Shining Pony, Baltimore, BrickHouse Books, 2013.

Long Trail Winding: New & Collected Upstate Stories, Sarasota, Goss Press, 2008.

Cherry Pie & Other Stories, Baltimore, Lite Circle Books,2001.

Eranos, (*Livre d'Artiste*) Baltimore, Goss Press, 2000.

In Foreign Parts, Delhi, Birch Brook Press, 1997.

Horse & Cart: Stories from the Country, Washington, D.C., The Wineberry Press, 1990.

Fire & Water: Six Stories, Van Nuys, Perivale Press, 1983.

III. DRAMA:

Impossible Interludes: Three Short Plays, Baltimore, BrickHouse Books, 2012.

IV. ART AND ARCHITECTURE:

Ten Large Etchings by Elisabeth Stevens, Sarasota, Goss Press, 2008.

Elisabeth Stevens' Guide to Baltimore's Inner Harbor, Baltimore, Stemmer House, 1981.

Artist of Delight: A Retrospective of the Works of Keith M. Martin, 1911-1983, Baltimore, George J. Ciscle Gallery, 1987.

Prints Today: A Short Guide to the Graphic Art Market, Washington, D.C., The Washington Print Club, 1971.

Jules Bissier, 1983-1965, New York, Lefebre Gallery, 1969.